JOHN D. MacDONALD

"One of the most exciting story writers of the day." *Pensacola News-Journal*

"The John O'Hara of the crime-suspense story." *The New York Times*

"Bestselling writer in the U.S." *Walter Winchell*

"An expert." *San Francisco News*

"An author whose swiftly paced, admirably characterized novels leave you breathless." *The Community Reporter*

NOW MEET HIS GREAT
CHARACTER—THAT UNCOMMON
HERO NAMED TRAVIS McGEE,
IN THIS COMPELLING STORY IN
THE BRILLIANT SERIES BY

JOHN D. MacDONALD

S0-BAW-266

Fawcett Gold Medal Books
in the Travis McGee Series
by John D. MacDonald

THE DEEP BLUE GOOD-BY   14176 $2.25
NIGHTMARE IN PINK   14259 $2.25
A PURPLE PLACE FOR DYING   14219 $2.25
THE QUICK RED FOX   14264 $2.25
A DEADLY SHADE OF GOLD   14221 $2.25
BRIGHT ORANGE FOR THE SHROUD   14243 $2.25
DARKER THAN AMBER   14162 $2.25
ONE FEARFUL YELLOW EYE   14146 $2.25
PALE GRAY FOR GUILT   14148 $2.25
THE GIRL IN THE PLAIN BROWN WRAPPER   14256 $2.25
DRESS HER IN INDIGO   14170 $2.25
THE LONG LAVENDER LOOK   13834 $2.25
A TAN AND SANDY SILENCE   14220 $2.25
THE SCARLET RUSE   13952 $2.25
THE TURQUOISE LAMENT   14200 $2.25
THE DREADFUL LEMON SKY   14148 $2.25
THE EMPTY COPPER SEA   14149 $2.25
THE GREEN RIPPER   14345 $2.50

Buy them at your local bookstore or use this handy coupon for ordering.

COLUMBIA BOOK SERVICE (a CBS Publications Co.)
32275 Mally Road, P.O. Box FB, Madison Heights, MI 48071

Please send me the books I have checked above. Orders for less than 5
books must include 75¢ for the first book and 25¢ for each additional
book to cover postage and handling. Orders for 5 books or more postage
is FREE. Send check or money order only.

Cost $_____   Name _____

Sales tax*_____   Address _____

Postage_____   City _____

Total $_____   State _____ Zip _____

* The government requires us to collect sales tax in all states except AK,
DE, MT, NH and OR.

This offer expires 1 November 81

8999

a purple place
for dying

by john d. macdonald

an original gold medal book

FAWCETT GOLD MEDAL • NEW YORK

A PURPLE PLACE FOR DYING

Published by Fawcett Gold Medal Books, a unit of CBS Publications, the Consumer Publishing Division of CBS Inc.

All characters in this book are fictional and any resemblance to persons living or dead is purely coincidental.

Copyright © 1964 by John D. MacDonald

ISBN: 0-449-14219-1

All rights reserved, including the right to reproduce this book or portions thereof.

Printed in the United States of America

31 30 29 28 27 26 25

a purple place
for dying

SHE TOOK THE CORNER too fast, and it was definitely not much of a road. She drifted it through the corner on the gravel, with one hell of a drop at our left, and then there was a big rock slide where the road should have been. She stomped hard and the drift turned into a rough sideways skid, and I hunched low expecting the white Alpine to trip and roll. But we skidded all the way to the rock and stopped with inches to spare and a great big three feet between the rear end and the drop-off. The skid had killed the engine.

"What a stinking nuisance!" Mona Yeoman said.

The cooling car made tinkling sounds. A noisy bird laughed at us. A lizard sped through the broken rock.

"End of the line?"

"Goodness, no. We can walk it from here. It's a half mile, I guess. I haven't been up here in ever so long."

"How about my gear?"

"It didn't seem to me you had very much. I guess you might as well bring it along, Mr. McGee. Perhaps you might be able to roll enough of this rock over the edge so you can get the jeep by. Or I can send some men to do it."

"If we're going to keep this as quiet as possible, I better give it a try."

"That makes sense."

"If I decide to try to help you, Mrs. Yeoman."

She glanced at me. Her eyes were the beautiful blue of robins' eggs, and had just about as much expression. "You've come this far, haven't you? I think you will."

I lifted my suitcase out of the little car, and we climbed over the rock. It was a fresh slide. The broken edges of the rock showed that. I felt just as happy to be out of the car. The road was steep and the curves were very interesting. She had met me at noon at an airport fifty miles away, quite a distance from her home base. She said she had a

7

place I could stay, a very hidden place, and we could do all our talking after we got there. Ever since meeting her I had been trying to figure her out.

She did not seem to fit either the rough country or the type of clothing she was wearing. She was a big ripe-bodied blonde of about thirty. She had a lot of control, and a competent way of handling herself, and a mild invulnerable arrogance. She would have looked far more at home on Park Avenue and Fifty-Something, in the highest of high style on a Sunday afternoon, wearing a fantastic hat and walking a curly little blue dog.

Here she strode up the gravel road in six-stitch boots, twill trousers, a tweed hacking coat, a sand-pale cowgirl hat. Though we were high, there was no wind and the sun made walking very hot work. I stopped and put my suitcase down and took my suit coat off.

"Good idea," she said, and shed hers and slung it over her shoulder. She went on, with the air that she was destined to walk ahead with most of the world following in single file. Her waist was narrow and she held her back very straight. The pale twill pants, a shade darker than her hat, were almost as tight as her skin. I read female character from sterns. Hers was hefty, shapely, rich and unapproachable. This one, I decided, would consider any gift of her favors a truly earth-shaking event, to be signaled by rare wine, incense and silk sheets. And she had the look of almost being able to live up to her own billing.

She was intent on one thing at a time. Walk now. Talk later.

The road ended at a cabin. It was on a half acre of naturally level ground, a rocky shelf three-quarters of the way up the mountain. The cabin was of silver-gray wood, twenty feet square, old but honestly made, with a steep roof. There was an open shed beside it containing cords of wood and an ancient jeep still wearing its army paint. There was a shack behind it, against the rock face of the hill. There was a privy built out over one hell of a drop.

I followed her up onto the porch and she pried a key out of the pocket of those tight pants and unlocked the door.

"This is the bunk room and living room. That fireplace heats it beautifully. Kitchen through there. Wood stove. A good stock of staples. There's a spring up the hill. That's very rare around here. The water is piped into the kitchen. Cold water only. Excellent water though. I assume you saw the outside plumbing. The battery in the jeep is probably dead, but it should start if you run it downhill. You can take it to a gas station and see what it needs and put the amount on your bill. There are some rough clothes in that closet there. I doubt there's anything big enough to fit you, Mr. McGee, but I think you can make do."

"Mrs. Yeoman?"

"There are no sheets but plenty of blankets and . . . What?"

"I am not buying the place. I am not even renting it. Maybe I'm not even staying. So let's get to it, shall we?"

She looked at me with disapproval. "But somebody *has* to help me," she said. "Why did you come so far if . . ."

"Like a self-respecting call girl, Mrs. Yeoman, I reserve the right to pick and choose. Once upon a time a lady assumed I'd happily kill somebody for her. That isn't my line of work."

"This is nothing like that! Fran Weaver is one of my oldest friends. She said that if anybody in the world could . . ."

"I know. I know. She wrote me. I got in touch. You sent plane fare. You gambled your money, and I gambled my time. Now we see if we can get together." I put my suitcase on the bunk and opened it and took out the bottle carrier. "Bourbon with no ice?"

"Please. Some water, half and half. You'll find the water cold enough."

It ran rusty at first and cleared quickly, and it was cold enough to numb my fingers. I put drinks in two mismatched glasses and took them in. She sat on a leather cushion on the raised hearth. It was cooler inside. She had put her jacket around her shoulders and laid her hat aside.

I sat in a thong chair nearby. She lifted her glass and said, "To an agreement."

"Fine." We drank and I said, "I took this one blind because I'm almost broke, Mrs. Yeoman."

She looked concerned. "That . . . isn't very heartening."

"Like not being successful? I'm very successful."

"I don't understand."

"I work when the money gets low. Otherwise I enjoy my retirement, Mrs. Yeoman. I'm taking it in installments, while I'm young enough to enjoy it. I am commonly known as a beach bum. I live on a houseboat. I live as well as I want to live, but sometimes I have to go to work. Reluctantly. Do you understand the terms?"

"I . . . I think so. Fran said . . ."

"Something has to have been taken from you, something

that belongs to you. You have exhausted all ways of getting it back. I'll make a try at it, if I go for the situation. If I can make a recovery, I keep half the value."

"It . . . it couldn't work that way in my case."

"Then let's walk back down that hill."

"No. Wait a minute. Let me tell you the situation. My father was Cubitt Fox. That doesn't mean anything to you, I know. But it is still a remembered name around here. I was his only child. My mother died two years after I was born. He tried to raise me like he would a son. He died twenty years ago, when I was twelve. He was forty-four. His dearest and closest friend was Jasper Yeoman. Jass was thirty-eight when daddy died. The will named Jass executor. He took over. He was very kind and generous. I went to good schools in the east, Mr. McGee. After I graduated from Vassar, I went to work in New York, on a magazine. I was on a generous allowance. I was twenty-two. I fell in love with a married man. We ran away together. It was a ghastly and horrible mistake. In Paris he had a change of heart and went scurrying back to his wife. I stayed there, for almost a year. I did too much drinking and I did some very foolish things. Then I got sick. Jass came over. He took me to Switzerland and stayed with me until I was well. I needed emotional stability and security and affection. Jass and I were married aboard ship on the way back, nine years ago. He's fifty-eight now. Up until a year ago, it was . . . a comfortable life. Jass is a rich and successful and tough-minded man. It was a first marriage for him. We've been unable to have children, and it's my fault, not his. A year ago I fell in love again. I thought Jass would be . . . reasonable. He hasn't been. I decided I would leave him. I thought I would get the money my father left me and leave him. I was still getting the allowance which I thought was the interest from the estate held in trust for me. I know there were several trust funds. I had been receiving fifteen hundred dollars a month since I was twenty-one. And spending it. I've been a little too damned good at spending it. Jass was the executor, as I told you. I asked for an accounting. He laughed at me. He said that my father's estate had been used up years ago, and that he had been continuing my allowance out of his own pocket. I demanded to see the figures. He said that they wouldn't mean anything to me if I saw them. He said daddy had made foolish investments, and the estate money had run out at the time we were married.

"Mr. McGee, my father was successful! At the time he died the papers said that his estate, before taxes, was worth over two million dollars. It couldn't be gone. I think my husband has . . . taken all that money somehow."

"Mrs. Yeoman, I think you need a lawyer and an accountant. I don't think you need me."

"Let me tell you a few facts of life. This is Esmerelda County. Eight miles down the valley is the City of Esmerelda. In the city is the Esmerelda Bank and Trust Company. My husband is the county and the city and the bank, and he is a lot of other things. Jass goes on hunting trips with the other men who run this whole state. He plays poker with them. Damn it, I am being treated like a child bride, as if this was some sort of little temper tantrum. I'm supposed to be a good girl and get over it."

"But did you see a lawyer?"

"I couldn't find a lawyer in Esmerelda who wanted to touch it. I found a young lawyer in Belasco, over in the next county. He poked around for a month. I can't remember all he said, but I think I can remember the important parts. My husband had to give an account of his . . . his stewardship to the probate judge, and file reports with the court, because I was a minor, I guess. He made three reports, five years after daddy died, and ten years after, and fifteen years after. The last was a final report, five years ago, claiming the estate was exhausted. The judge is dead. Four years ago they built the new courthouse. The records are in the dead files and they aren't even indexed, and there's no way of telling if the records are there or not. The lawyer Jass used is dead, and nobody knows where his files and records went to. My lawyer said he would have to start from the other end, to get a copy of the tax statement filed with the federal government twenty years ago, and identify the assets, and then trace them through the public records of sales and so forth, and build up a case that some kind of funny business had gone on. Then I would have to bring action against my husband. Even if we got something to go on, he said Jass could stall for three or four years before we could ever get it into court. In the meantime, my allowance has been cut off until I, quote, come to my senses, unquote. He pats me on the head and tells me to forget all this nonsense."

"Maybe the estate wasn't as big as you thought it was, Mrs. Yeoman."

"Oh, come now! Daddy loved land. He had faith in the future of this area. I showed the lawyer, and I can show you, just *one* of the pieces he owned. Now it's got the Chem-Del plant on it, and two big shopping centers and about four hundred tract houses. He checked it out in the County Clerk's office, and it wasn't sold to pay estate taxes. The records show it was sold three years after he died to something called the Apex Development Corporation. The records in the state capital show that Apex lasted four years and collapsed, with no asset values. Daddy owned this area right here, too. Ten thousand acres. Jass knew I loved this place. He gave me a deed to this part of it, nine hundred acres, for my birthday about seven years ago. He said he bought it back from the people who owned it. Four months ago I looked into the idea of selling it, but Jass is on the deed too, and I can't."

"What do you think you want from me?"

"The estate was stolen from me, by my husband. There must be some way of . . . of making him make restitution. Some way of making him take me seriously. Because I am serious, damn it. I want my money, and I want a divorce, and I want to marry John Webb."

"The money is necessary, I assume."

"John hasn't any, if that's what you mean. He's an assistant professor at State Western. The legislature controls the University. Jass has good friends in the legislature. The day I leave him, according to Jass, John Webb gets booted out with damn small chance of getting a job elsewhere. I've been reduced to . . . to being a captive, Mr. McGee."

"A smart woman can make a man feel happy to be rid of her."

"I have been an absolute bitch for months. He laughs at me. He says I'll get over it. He's always been . . . very ardent. I haven't let him touch me. That doesn't seem to bother him either. I think he has somebody else. He is so terribly confident I'll get over this little tantrum, and be his girl bride again. I had to sell jewelry to pay that lawyer, and I had to sell jewelry to pay for your plane ticket. He says once I prove to him that I want to be a wife again, we can go back to the way things used to be. I told my troubles to Fran when she visited me. And you were the only thing she could suggest."

"I don't see how there's anything which can be done."

"Mr. McGee, I want to be realistic about this. I've scaled

my wants way way down. I want him convinced he should let me go, and I want to walk away with fifty thousand dollars. If you can pry me loose somehow, with a hundred thousand, I'll give you half. If you can manage more, I'll give you ten percent of everything over a hundred thousand. My only other choice is to sit around and wait for him to die. And he is a very healthy man."

"Or you could just take off with this Webb."

She made a face. "I threatened that. He said he would never divorce me for desertion. He said he would send people to find me and bring me back. And those people would give John Webb a whipping for wife-stealing. John isn't very strong, physically. No. He has to want to let me go."

She stood up and paced restlessly. She had a lot of vitality, a lot of gloss and bounce and directed energy. She didn't look like the kind you can quell and keep and humble.

"Why would he take your money?"

"I think I have that figured out. I heard some rumors. When I was about fifteen, beginning about then, he had some very bad years. He's always been bold, in a business way. I guess he got too bold. He overextended himself in too many directions, so that when things started to go bad for him, he didn't have enough money to move around. So he had to dig into mine to save himself. Maybe he thought he would pay it back, but he had to take more and more of it, and do a lot of shifty work before he could stem the tide and start to get healthy again. I guess by then it seemed easier to fake a lot of things and close out the estate rather than try to pay it back. And the best way to cover it all up was to marry me. When there was a chance of marrying me, he took it. I don't think he ever really wanted to be married. He isn't that sort of a man. It was something he had to do to protect himself. I was in ghastly shape, and I jumped at the chance. During the years when . . . it seemed pretty good, I never did really have the status of a wife. He didn't change his way of life at all. Or ever seem to take me seriously."

"I just don't see where I have any approach I can use."

"Mr. McGee, he didn't pull these tricky things in a complete vacuum, you know. He does make enemies. Somebody must have enough on him to . . . to be able to put pressure on him. And I don't think Jass is as casual and confident about this as he would like to have me believe. I'm pretty sure people have been following me. I think I do worry him a little. I suppose it would look bad if the newspapers picked it up—Jass Yeoman's wife demanding an accounting of what happened to her father's money. I guess he must have been worried that maybe I had squirreled away some of my allowance."

"What makes you think that?"

"I had a nice little Mexican maid for five years. She quit six months ago and got married. Two men went to her and questioned her for hours, mostly about my personal finances, how much I spent and on what and so on. They claimed to be some sort of accountants. Afterwards she worried about it for a few days, and then came and told me. That happened just two months ago. I had . . . an unusual relationship with Dolores. We confided in each other. She was very dear to me."

"And you think that because your husband might be worried, he might be susceptible to some kind of pressure."

"If I knew what to do, Mr. McGee, I would have tried to do it myself. I even thought I might blackmail my own husband. I hired a man to find out about other women. I guess he was clumsy. The police threw him in jail for three nights running, for little things like spitting on the sidewalk. He gave up."

"I just don't know," I said.

She asked me to follow her. We went out to the barren edge of the dropoff. The crumpled hills around us were red-brown, with little patches of stubborn green. There was a clump of wind-twisted pines nearby. She pointed west. The range we were on cascaded down and flattened out, and across the semi-desert plain, distorted by heat shimmer, misty in the distance, we could see the city of Esmerelda, pale cubes rising out of a cluttered smear. She pointed out U.S. 87 angling toward the city from the northeast, about four miles away and three or four thousand feet lower than we were. I could make out two big silver transport trucks crawling along amid the swifter beetles of private cars.

She stood bareheaded, half facing me. "I'm thirty-two years old, Mr. McGee. There's been a lot of wasted time and wasted years. I'm grateful to him, in a way. But I want out. I'm the captive princess, and that's the castle down there. Jass is the king. I can have a little freedom of motion, as long as I ride back to the castle walls at nightfall. Corny, I guess. But when you are in love you get some romantic images. And I'm not too ancient to cry myself to sleep. I must have help."

She stood at my right, half turned to face me, the sun heat of the still day misting her forehead and her upper lip. She wanted the answer. And I frowned in silence, searching for the words to tell her that this was not my sort of thing.

Suddenly she plunged forward, her shoulder brushing me and knocking me back. She went with her head tilted back, and she landed face down on the baked dirt and the edges of stone, and slid at least six inches after she struck, without having lifted her hands to try to break her fall. The noise that started the fall was a curiously ugly noise. It was a dull sound of impact, like the sound of burying a hatchet into a soft and rotten stump. She lay without twitch, without sound, totally soft and flattened. I heard then the distant ringing bark of a heavy rifle, a *ka-rang*, echoing in the still rock hills of the windless day. There was too much open space between me and the cabin. I ran in a very fast and very random pattern toward the pines fifty feet away, skidded around them and fell, clutching a twisted root, my legs hanging half over the edge of the drop. A dislodged stone clattered and bounced once, then hit long seconds later and far away. I swallowed the gagging lump that was the clear visual memory of the wet hole punched high in her spine, through the silk blouse, dead center, about two inches below where her neck joined her good shoulders. A big caliber. Plenty of impact. Foot pounds of energy is a product of mass and velocity. Good velocity, for the sound to come that much later. A full second? Less. Five hundred yards? I pulled myself forward and peered around the trunk of the tree. An empty jumble of hills over there, a thousand crouching-places.

I had to settle myself down to a rational appraisal of his luck. He had the whole torso to go for. Provided it wasn't some halfwit potting at a twig. That much slug, in shoulder or hip, would do the job. Even if he'd gotten the thigh or the upper arm, my chance of getting help to her in time would have been slim. He had exploded that big pipe that held all the circuits. Massive hydrostatic pressure on the spinal fluid, blowing the brain dark in a microsecond.

She had died without knowing she was dead.

I looked at her, my eyes at ground level. The top of her head was toward me. Once I had seen a fence-jumping mare killed by a pickup truck. The corner post of the windshield had hit her behind the ear and snapped her neck, and she had gone down in the same utterly final and boneless way.

I watched the crumpled country of that neighbor mountain, saw nothing, heard nothing. In the silence I thought I heard a car start, a long long way off.

The princess wouldn't be making it back to the castle tonight.

When I got tired of waiting, I scrambled up and ran for the cabin in the way Uncle had taught me once upon a time. I dived into the cool interior, and let my precious treasured flesh unpucker. Her empty glass was on the hearth, pink lipstick on the rim. The leather cushion still bore the imprint of that round behind. I saw battered binoculars hanging on a nail. Eight power. Navy issue. The left lens was knocked out of true. The right was good enough. It showed me the flies with the bright green back-ends scurrying around on her silk shirt.

Her leather purse was on the chair with the jacket and cowgirl hat. I found eighty-nine dollars in it. I took the eighty. I put my bottle back in the suitcase, went to the doorway, took three deep breaths, then went running for the road. I ran until I was down around the first curve. I watched my fingers shake as I lit a cigarette. And then I went swinging down the road.

two

WHEN I CLAMBERED over the rock slide, I had the insane feeling I should start turning the rocks over, looking for the little white car. I squatted. The gravel was too loose to take a print, and where there wasn't gravel, the earth was baked too hard. But I could see where the little car had been backed around and driven away. I had remembered her leaving the keys in it. There had been no reason not to. Two or three miles down the hill was the weathered gate I had opened and then closed again after she had driven the car through.

I wondered if it had been her car I had heard starting up. I had another idea. I left my suitcase on the road and climbed to the top of the slide. It took me about five minutes to find the place—scorched blackened rock and a faint stink of explosive. All somebody had to do was pick a likely crack, wedge a couple of sticks in there, and tumble a few tons of rock onto the road. Why? To make her leave the car there and walk in? Why? So somebody could take the car? Why?

I ran out of answers, and picked up my suitcase and continued on down the mountain. I thought how curiously merciless it is to kill a provocative woman. They aren't supposed to be killed. No one is supposed to render useless all that sweet flesh and heat and honeyed membrane.

But dead she was, and dead she would forever be. So I occupied myself with devising and double-checking a reasonable story. After I had let myself out the weathered gate, I was on narrow, pitted concrete, a small road which went nowhere very important, and was in no hurry to get there. I headed back the way we had come. I estimated it another two miles, but it could be further. I had hopes of being picked up. But the four cars that passed me, going my way, went by so quickly I couldn't even get a decent glance at the people in them.

At last I came to the vaguely-remembered crossroads, to a dusty gas station and lunchroom, surrounded by broken pieces of automobile. A man sat in the shade in a chair tilted against the front of the gas station. I did not disturb his siesta.

I went into the lunchroom. A stocky young girl in a soiled green jumper sat at a table reading a fan magazine. She got up slowly when the screen door creaked. She had enormous breasts and she looked like Buddy Hackett.

"I just want to use the phone."

She didn't answer. She just let herself plump back down into the chair.

"What's this place called? So I can direct somebody."

"Garry's at Cotton Corners."

I got out my dime and looked in the front of the book. Police emergency, dial 119.

"Sheriff's department. Deputy London."

"I'm at Garry's place at Cotton Corners. I want to report a shooting and the theft of a motor vehicle."

"It happen there?"

"No. But I can take you to where it did happen."

"What's your name?"

"McGee. Travis McGee." I was aware of the rigid attention of the girl behind me.

"I can have a car there in about ten minutes. You wait right there. You got a description of the stolen vehicle?"

"A white Sunbeam Alpine convertible. Local plates."

"Know the number?"

"No."

"Driver?"

"I have no idea."

"Where did it happen?"

"In the hills about five or six miles from here. I walked out. So it happened well over an hour ago, closer to two hours."

"Who got hurt?"

"A woman named Mrs. Jasper Yeoman. She's dead."

"Mrs. Yeoman! Good God almighty! You wait there."

I hung up. The stocky girl looked adoringly at me. "Wow!" she said. "How about that! Son of a bitch!"

"How about a coke?"

"Sure. Coming up. Hey, what happened? Who shot her?"

"Do you know who she is?"

"Who doesn't? She's bought gas here lots of times. Her

old man, he owned half Esmerelda County. She was a stuck-up bitch. Who did it?"

"I better let the police ask the questions."

"Did you *see* it happen?"

"Easy on the ice, please."

She banged the glass down in front of me and went trotting out. I heard her jabbering at the man who'd been asleep. They both came back in. He was younger than I had thought. He was dried brown, like the rock lizards. He looked at me as if we had just shared some obscene joke. "That big bitch is dead for sure, ha?"

God, the pleasure they take in it, the excited joy in finding out that death can chop down the tall ones too, can fell the money tree. They both looked at me as if I'd brought them candy, and I told them she was dead indeed.

"You not from around here," he said. It wasn't a question. "She was old Cube Fox's daughter. My daddy worked for Cube for a time. Cube didn't marry until he was past thirty. She was his only legal child, but you can bet your ass there's anyway forty grownup people running around this end of the state with Cube's blue eyes, and the rest of them Mex. Cube was plain death on Mex gals. He talked the language good. Cube and Jass Yeoman, they used to run together. My daddy said when Jass married Cube's daughter, he bet Cube was spinning in that grave saying curses to wilt the grass overhead. Who killed her, Mister?"

"I'm a stranger around here."

A car rolled up and somebody gave the siren one little touch so that it made a low fading growl.

We went out. It was a pale gray sedan with an obscure decal on the door. Two men in crisp faded khaki got out. They wore television hats and gun belts, silver badges. Nothing seems authentic any more. In the retirement villages the old coots from Upper Berth, Ohio, wear Marshal Dillon pants and squint themselves into authentic weather wrinkles in the bake of the sun.

" 'Lo, Arnie," the bigger one said.

"Hi, Homer. Hi, Dave."

Homer stuck his thumbs in his belt, indicated me with a jerk of his head and said, "You heard him on the phone, didn't you? You and Sis?"

"Sure did. And if it isn't the goddamdest . . ."

"Arnie, you or Sis might get on that phone there and pick up one of them ten or twenty-five dollar awards from the

Eagle or from KEAG-TV. Then we'd sure as hell find you are about four feet shy of having the legal set-back here. And you never heard of the sign ordinance. And the county will find out you got a dirty grill and dirty glasses. And all that junk around looks to me like an attractive nuisance."

"Homer, if you want me and Sis to keep shut about this, all you got to do is say so."

"Arnie, if you or Sis should run nine miles into the scrub and whisper this to a gopher, I'll have you working the roads and Sis on laundry, so help me." He turned his back on them and said, "McGee?"

"That's right."

"I'm Hardy and this here is Dave Carlyle. We'll wait for the Sherf. He'll be right along. He'll be the one to ask questions. Meanwhile, hold onto the back of your neck with both hands."

I did as told. The search was quick and professional. Belt, belly, groin, armpits, hip pockets and ankles.

"Got anything with you?"

"Suitcase inside."

"Bring it out, Dave."

The smaller and older deputy brought it out. He put it on the hood of the sedan, opened it, pawed through it, closed it up.

"Identification now," Homer Hardy said. "Don't give me your wallet. Just a driver's license, if you have one."

He put it on the hood of the car, copied information into his notebook, handed it back. "Thank you, Mr. McGee."

"You're welcome."

"Hairy comes," Dave Carlyle said. A dusty new station wagon came at high speed, slewed in and stopped in a thick cloud of fine dust. Homer turned to the couple and said, "Get on in there, you."

They went reluctantly. The Sheriff got out of his car. He was younger than his two deputies. He had a massive chest, squared-off jaw, bull neck, the look of the one-time athlete in one of the contact sports. He wore a faded White Sox baseball cap, a blue and white checked sports shirt worn outside his gray slacks. I guessed he was growing a little belly and made it less conspicuous by wearing his shirts outside his pants.

"Well?" he said to Homer.

"This man is Travis D. McGee, Fort Lauderdale, Florida. He's clean, and there's just clothes and toilet stuff and one opened bottle of bourbon in his bag there. No objection at all to search. I put a lid on Arnie and Sis and it will stick. We haven't asked this man a thing, so you know as much right now as we do about the rest of it."

"He'll come with me and you follow along," the Sheriff said. Dave put my suitcase in the station wagon. I got in with the Sheriff. He told me his name was Buckelberry. He said it without a smile. I wondered if he had gotten all that neck and shoulders by objecting to any cracks about his name.

"Where do we go?"

"Turn here and go about three miles and there's a gate . . ."

"Up at the old cabin, eh? I know the place." He started up quickly. "Who shot her?"

"I don't know. It was a sniper. A heavy rifle at long range, Sheriff. It hit her high in the spine, from the rear and killed her instantly. I left her where she fell. I couldn't see anybody. I couldn't help her in any way. And I didn't exactly want to give some nut a chance at me if he was still around."

"When did it happen?"

"I didn't think to look at my watch until I would estimate ten minutes had passed. My best guess would be the shot was fired at two twenty-five. I took cover. I waited around for about thirty minutes. Then I came down the road to where we'd left her car."

"The road goes to the cabin."

"Not with a rock slide across it. We had to leave the car a half mile down the road and walk. When I got back the car was gone. I remembered noticing she'd left the key in it when we left it there. I walked out. I couldn't get a ride. I walked all the way to Cotton Corners. There was no way I could get in touch any sooner than I did."

"Stray shot?"

"It's a possibility, I suppose."

"You hear the shot?"

"Yes. The slug knocked her down very quick and hard, and I heard it just as she came to rest, so I would guess it was less than a second later."

We had come to the gate. The other car stopped behind us. Dave hustled ahead and got the gate and left it open. We headed up the gravel road.

"Now where do you fit in this, Mr. McGee?"

"Through a mutual friend. Fran Weaver. Mrs. Hyde Weaver, a widow, an old friend of Mona Yeoman. She visited Mona a while back. I've wanted a place where I could complete a project, and have total privacy, and keep expenses down at the same time. Fran suggested Mona's cabin. I got in touch and she agreed to loan it to me. I flew in at noon today. She met me at Carson and drove me to the cabin. She showed me the place. It was agreeable to both of us. I was to have the use of the jeep. With a pry bar and a little sweat I could clear that rock slide. We went out to the edge of the drop there. She wanted to show me the view. And all of a sudden the slug knocked her down dead."

"Why Carson instead of Esmerelda?"

"I have no idea. She suggested it. Maybe she had an errand over there."

We came to the rock slide. He pulled as far over to the right as he could get, and the other car stopped beside us.

"Call for an ambulance?" Dave asked out his open window.

"Let's take a look first, boys. What kind of project, Mr. McGee?"

"It's an operating manual for pleasure boats."

"Writing one? Damned dry place to come to write about the water."

"If Mona and I could reach an understanding, I was going to have my stuff shipped here. It's all crated up." I sighed. "It would have been a nice quiet place to work."

We climbed over the loose rock and walked up the road. Buckelberry and I were in the lead. I was getting a little tired of that road. It was nearly five o'clock. I was definitely getting tired of walking. When we came around the last bend, I saw the roof peak of the cabin. We went up the last twenty feet of slope and I said, beginning to point, "She's right over . . ."

I stopped and stared at the absolutely bare expanse of sun-baked earth and rock. The three of them stared at me. I felt my mouth stretch into a foolish, apologetic smile. "The body *was* right over there, I swear."

They shrugged. We walked over. I realized there would be blood. I knew that slug had gone through her, and blown a pretty good hole in front. I knew right where she had gone down. I sat on my heels. There was a place there that looked as if dirt and stone had been scooped out and the area patted flat again, but I couldn't be certain. I looked at the drop. If anybody had scooped the stained earth out of there and heaved it over the edge, it was gone for good.

I stood up and said heartily, "Well, she left stuff in the cabin."

We went to the cabin. The door was locked. "When I left, Sheriff, I left this door open."

Three faces stared at me with heavy skepticism. Buckelberry shrugged and began to feel around on the porch joists. After a few minutes he found a key and looked at it, fingered the mat of cobwebs off it. "You opened it with this key, McGee?"

"She had a key with her."

We went inside. It had the flavor of having been empty for months. Hat, purse and jacket were gone. The glasses were gone. The leather cushion was back on a chair. I remembered snapping a cigarette into the fireplace. Mrs. Yeoman had not smoked. I crouched and looked for my cigarette. That was gone.

"Now what the hell?" Buckelberry said irritably.

I described her car. I described exactly how she was dressed. I told them just where the bullet had hit her, and what it had sounded like.

They stood and stared at me. Buckelberry winked at Homer Hardy.

Homer said, "I see what you meant, Sherf, about not calling for the ambulance."

"Go on out and rest yourself in the shade, boys," Buckelberry said.

They went out. I heard Homer laugh. Buckelberry told me to sit down. He sat on the bunk. "This was a damn fool idea, McGee."

"I don't know what you're talking about."

"Why, that fool woman has been threatening to run off with a college teacher for months. She's been after old Jass for months to turn her loose. Jass has been kidding around town, telling people it's no worse than a bad case of the trots. She'll get over it, he says. And Mona knows well enough that she could never get so far Jass couldn't have her brought back, and give her a good whipping when he gets her back. She's just got a little passing case of the hot pants, McGee. Now what were we supposed to do? Spend a week crawling all over this up and down country looking for a body that isn't there? You did good, McGee. You had me almost believing you. You know, this is the sort of thing they tell me her daddy, old Cube Fox, used to pull, only he did it better."

"You're not making any sense, Sheriff."

"I'll tell you what makes sense. She's got foolish friends who would try to pry her loose from Jass Yeoman. That little car is stuffed off in the brush someplace. She and her teacher are hightailing it out of here by now. She's scared of Jass and she wanted to get the best head start she could. If we thought her dead, it might give her another week to get hid good and take the edge off that case of hot pants. But it doesn't work. Soon as we get down to the car I'll get hold of Jass. Eight to five he has her right back home tomorrow or the next day. And she'll be eating off high places for two weeks once he gets through welting that fancy tail of hers. What are you anyhow? Some kind of actor friend from her New York days?"

"Are you a good Sheriff?"

His eyes went small. "It isn't an elective office in this county."

"It shouldn't be an elective office anywhere. Amen to that. So think like a good law man. If that was the scheme, where is the trimming?"

"What?"

"If it was a cute trick, wouldn't anybody with a grain of sense plant some kind of misleading evidence? Animal blood. Some sign of a struggle. A button off her clothes. Something, for God's sake, to make it look better."

Little ripples of muscle ran along the line of that square jaw. "I can play that game too. Maybe no evidence makes it look better because you'd then be able to say what you just said."

"That's like the game of guessing which hand the pebble is in. I know one thing, Sheriff. I saw her go down. We can play a lot of guessing games. But I saw her dead."

He shook his head. "I don't want to be hard on a man trying to do a favor for a friend. I could book you for malicious mischief, I guess. Next time I see Miz Yeoman, I'll tell her you gave it a good try."

"Do you have good lab people?"

"Got the use of them, McGee. We got a central CID for the neighboring ten counties."

"Why don't you turn them loose around here?"

"Don't give up, do you? There's no need for that. We'll have a line on that pair by midnight. From here they run one of three ways. Vegas, Mexico or New York. Old Jass will reach out a great long arm with a little snap hook on the end of it and he will pull her right back home. Come on. Let's get out of here." We went out into the late slant of October sunlight, soon to slide behind the big mountains far beyond Esmerelda.

"The way I see it, it's Jass's fault," he said. "He let her range too far and wide before he brought her back and tried to settle her down. She could have got all the education she ever needed within fifty mile of home, and that's the way it would have been for her if Cube lived. But I guess Jass wanted her fancied up."

We all trudged back down to the cars. I heard Homer and Dave muttering to each other, snickering from time to time. Everybody seemed to be so damned certain of everything, I decided not to send them up that rock slide to find the place where somebody had planted the charge to blow it down.

Sheriff Buckelberry sent Homer and Dave back onto patrol. He called in and asked his communications to give him a phone hookup to Jasper Yeoman, then changed his mind. "Too many unauthorized people tuned in on this net," he explained to me. "No need to start them all laughing."

"If I had to guess the weapon," I said, "I would say about a .44 Magnum. If a man had taken a full swing with an eight-pound sledge and hit her right between the shoulders, it would have about the same effect. A smaller caliber would have given more penetration and less impact, Sheriff."

"For God's sake, McGee!"

"There can't be too many people around with that much gun."

"There aren't, and the ones that have them don't go around bagging blonde wives, boy. I'm going into town. That suit you?"

"I guess it has to. I would appreciate it if you could drop me at a motel. Something not too far out of town, clean and cheap if those two things go together around here."

"You going to stay long?"

"I might ask Mr. Yeoman if I can use that cabin."

"Don't try to get any cuter than you are."

"What does that mean, Sheriff?"

"This is a friendly enough place. We don't have a hard-nose police routine, county or city. We don't need it. But if a good citizen like Mr. Yeoman should mention that he isn't fond of you, we'd have to sharpen your heels and drive you down into hard ground. I guess it's old-fashioned. The people who pay a hell of a lot of taxes get a hell of a lot of service."

We came out onto Route 87 and turned left. The sun was gone from the valley floor, but the afterglow made the tall pale buildings of Esmerelda look pink. The divided highway ran arrow straight into the city. He pulled into a place called the Latigo Motel, said it was cheap and clean, told me to stay out of trouble, let me out and drove off.

The motel was built on a narrow plot, and extended at right angles to the highway, trapped between the Idle Hour Lanes and the Baby Giant Soop-R-Mart. In the cool blue dusk they had turned the red floodlights on in their little cactus garden. Across the highway was the Corral Diner—Choice Western Beef, and up the line was the ChunkyBurger Drivein, their juke audible for great distances over the groaning of trucks. A fat and absent-minded young woman with a baby riding her big soft hip, checked me into number seven and took my five dollars plus tax, and came out of her daze when she found out I didn't have a car. She had difficulty comprehending that. She looked awed. I was a true eccentric.

I went down to seven. There was an extremely small swimming pool beyond the units, with a high redwood fence for privacy. There were a dozen screaming children in the pool. The unit was small, clean and very bare. I shed my jacket and stretched out on the double bed.

When you can keep moving, when you have to keep moving, you can keep a lot of things at arm's length. But when you stop they come in at you. I had not liked Mona Fox Yeoman. She had seemed artificial, self-important. She had been provocative rather than seductive. A man cannot keep himself from making bedroom speculations. Her manner had given me the feeling that I would like to shake her up, to mat that twenty-five dollar hairdo, to really get to her and put her to such work she would forget that lady-of-the-manor style of hers. I had not expected to ever be able to, but it was the index of that kind of desire. Some women instigate a good ruffling.

So she was a big creamy bitch standing beside me in her tailored tight pants, and suddenly she was fallen cooling meat, and it was too damned fast. I had seen dead women. I had seen sudden expected death, and sudden unexpected death, but never before the sudden and unexpected death of a handsome woman. It struck deeper than I would have guessed it could. There was more to it than the fact of a horrid waste. I couldn't identify what there was about it that had rocked me so, and kept rocking me. Somehow it was identified with my own mortality, my own inevitable day to die. She had gone far past childhood, yet when she was down, she was Little Girl smashed, and closer to my heart dead than alive. Emotional necrophilia.

I had thought that I was in fine balance. I had had a very bad time and I had come out of it very slowly and tentatively, with a skull full of wraiths and remorses, with the blood dreams and the flying twitches, and I had come out of it with enough money for a McGee-style therapy—a slow and cautious adjustment to beer and sun, boats and laughs, some little sandy-rumped beach girls, some fish-stalking and beach-walking and moon-watching, some improvised houseboat parties, a little unwinding in St. Thomas and over at Deep Water Cay. And I thought I had crawled back into my own skin, beach-bum McGee, the big chopped-up, loosejointed, pale-eyed, wire-haired, walnut-hided rebel—unregimented, unprogrammed, unimpressed. I had even believed I had grown another little layer of hide over those places where I could be hurt.

So when I became aware of the imminent necessity to acquire funds—being almost down to that war fund I lay aside for the expenses of operation—I knew I was going to be cold and smart about it this time. No empathy, boy. No tears for anybody who goes down the chute. Pick a ripe one and work it for the cash money and come happily back to houseboat life aboard the Busted Flush, Slip F-18, Bahia Mar, Lauderdamndale.

I had two reasonable prospects lined up, and when the letter from Fran Weaver had come, I had three. And thought to check this one out first.

But suddenly that extra layer of hide was gone.

So forget it, McGee. List the reasons for forgetting it. I had the plane ticket back. No loss. The prospective client was dead. There was no way of making any money out of this one. Nobody to split with when I recovered what had been stolen. Whatever was going on, people were playing for keeps. You didn't like the woman anyway. Get a night's sleep. Get out of town.

But you'll never find out why.

Man, can you afford idle curiosity? Count all the dead cats.

But rigging that rock slide means a lot of careful planning. Then why hide all traces? What does that accomplish?

You idiot, you've got a perfectly good little problem to work on, with the old broad in Jacksonville whose stepson lifted her collection of gold coins.

That one will keep. It won't be expensive to handle. Just bend him until the coins start falling out. Four or five days of work.

There was another thing which made this less attractive by the moment. There was a little cold spot on my spine—between the shoulder blades, and high. I had been with her when it happened. She hadn't been to the cabin in a long time. Somebody knew she was going there. With me?

If the rifleman had wanted to take both of us, he could have blown my head off first, on the assumption a woman would not react as quickly, would have stood there, frozen in horror, just long enough. Why leave the stranger alive? Confusion factor?

Maybe the small value I had was now over. This could be a very unpleasant area, a dangerous climate. I vowed to take no lonely strolls through the hills, and to watch the hands of strangers, and not to sit with my back to a window.

Maybe it would be very good sense to just leave.

But if you don't futz with it, friend, maybe somebody will get away clean.

What are you, McGee? Guardian of public morality? People get away with things every hour of every day. Murder isn't *that* unique. First thing you know, you'll be leading parades. It's police business, and you have met a very competent policeman.

There was just one trouble with the running argument. I knew I had made up my mind. I knew just when and how I had made it up. It was when I had taken the eighty dollars from her purse. I hadn't taken it for me. I had taken it for her. I was just picking it up the way you pick up ammunition when you anticipate a fight.

Once I was willing to admit it to myself, I felt a little bit easier. But there was still a feeling of strain in my mind which bothered me. I wanted to be stable as all hell, but the world was on a slight tilt. It was like being yanked around an unexpected curve. You lean for a long time. My friend Meyer, the economist, says that cretins are the only humans who can be absolutely certain of their own sanity. All the rest of us go rocketing along rickety rails over spavined bridges and along the edge of bottomless gorges. The man who believes himself free of any taint of madness is a damned liar. The trouble is, you never know exactly what might tip you off those rails. And that memorable chunking sound of heavy lead into her vulnerable back, through her pretty silk blouse, had touched something way below my level of consciousness. It roiled something up down there, something fairly nasty and ancient and invisible.

I went out and found their ice machine and came back and fixed a drink in a tumbler that came in a little wax bag explaining that it had been Steem-Sterilized. It had a little flake of raspberry lipstick on the edge of it. Presumably that had been Steem-Sterilized too. I should report it to the Sheriff. The usual efficient process is for the room maid to wipe the glasses on the used bath towels of the previous guests and then pop them into those comforting little bags. Next she wipes the john seat with the same towels, then slips the paper ribbon onto it, acclaiming its astonishing sterility. Then, with the beds made, she goes trundling off, pushing her square-wheeled cart, kicking the doors of the sleepers, clearing her throat with a ringing whock-tooey into the shrubbery, screaming her early morning greetings to friends three blocks away.

With drink in hand I lounged against the headboard and resolutely pushed emotional considerations aside and tried to make some cold sense out of what had happened. Somebody had planned to kill her and had killed her. So why have a witness? Somebody had known what her movements would be. It did not seem very likely that she would tell her husband that she was meeting a stranger at Carson Airport at noon and driving him to the cabin. Yet she had the feeling she had been followed lately. What if when we had come upon the rock slide, she had turned around and found some other place for us to talk? Somebody had known her well enough to know how she would react. She had planned to confer with me at the cabin, so by God, that was where she would take me. If they had known she had planned I would stay there for a time, it was a good guess we would walk in. By then the sniper would have been in position. We had made it easier by going out to the edge and standing there. But in any event we would probably have stood still for him somewhere in the exposed area, before leaving.

One thing was reasonably evident. The one who fired the shot was not the same one who took the car. It would have taken far too long to circle that rugged country.

Once the woman fell, my actions were predictable. I would take cover, and after a while I would retreat to the car. Finding it gone, I would walk out. That would give him or them time to remove the evidence of murder.

Skipping for the moment the possible reasons for taking her away, where had they taken her? In all that baked and tumbled wasteland of chasm and jumbled stone, there were ten thousand hiding places within a mile of the cabin, either downhill or up. She could be wedged into a small place and covered with loose stone. Two days of that oven sun would bake and draw every ounce of moisture out of her tissues, turning her into forty pounds of dry leather and string and bone, shrunken inside the folds of the cowgirl tailoring.

Wouldn't it have made more sense for somebody to entice her to the cabin alone? Kill at a closer and more certain range? Be assured of no interruption? Why have a witness running around loose, insisting she was dead?

One thing seemed certain. When something has been planned, and makes no sense, some of the facts are missing. I wondered who could supply them. The unnamed lawyer from Belasco? John Webb? Dolores?

My window was open. The room was dark. I could hear the rip and whuffle of traffic on 87, the music from the drivein, a muffled clatter of pins from the Idle Hour Lanes. Children no longer yelped in the pool. The television next door was turned high. A couple walked by my window, the woman saying, ". . . nose running all day so you let her swim til she turns blue for God's sake, Harry . . ."

I turned on a light and shut the window and fiddled with the big window unit until I had it adjusted to send a vague panting of warm air into the room, accompanied by such a grinding and rattling and droning that all sounds of the outside world were gone. This is the new privacy, the wall of noise which provides the nerve-nibbling solitude of the machine shop.

I napped and awoke with stale mouth and grainy eyes to find it was almost nine o'clock. I had expected sleep to be a buffer, making the dead woman less vivid, but in my mind she plunged and fell, plunged and fell, undiminished. After I had snorted into handfuls of cold water and had brushed my teeth, I walked over to the Corral Diner. I bought the evening Esmerelda *Eagle*. I read it as I awaited my steak, sitting in one of the booths opposite the long counter. It was a booster sheet. Progress is wonderful. Esmerelda is wonderful. Housing booms. Second phase of slum clearance program approved. Kalko Products to be first to start construction in new industrial park. Northeast arterial will bring airport fifteen minutes closer to Downtown. Expert predicts double population in next nine years. Esmerelda coach predicts unbeaten season, biggest ground-gaining average in six county conference. School bond issue to pass by overwhelming margin.

With the rush over, the diner was quiet. Five young women came trooping in. A bowling team. They wore little white stretch shirts and short white pleated tennis skirts, and carried bright plastic bags of gear. In an arc across each back was embroidered P U R I T Y. Over their hearts were embroidered their names. Dot, Connie, Beth, Margo and Janice. They stacked their jackets and gear in one booth and squeezed into another. I could not determine if they were secretarial types or young housewives. Often they are both. Two of them looked meaty enough to be competent at the game. They got coffee first, and huddled with a great deal of snickering and gasping, muttering and laughter. They acted conspiratorial, and I heard a few clinks of glass against the edges of the heavy coffee cups and knew the gals were belting a few. It seemed they had won. They became aware of me. They whispered and sniggered, and the ones with their backs to me managed to turn to look beyond me with a vast innocence, then take the quick sharp look and turn back to lean heads together and make their jokes. Man alone, worth appraising. Brown-faced stranger, with shoulders big enough to interest them. I could tell by the shrill and almost hysterical quality of their whoops of laughter that the muttered comments were getting ever more bawdy. Then one of the chunky ones whispered for a long time and her audience dissolved into helpless laughter when she was done.

Suddenly I realized that the world is upside down in more ways than one. They were the hard-eyed group, the appraisers, the potential aggressors, the bunch of guys making the half-obvious pitch at the interesting stranger. They made me feel almost girlish. I realized there had been something of the same flavor in Mona's arrogance—the unconscious usurpation of the male tradition of aggression. Touch me on my terms, buddy.

The steak was fried, rubbery and without flavor. The potatoes were soggy. The lettuce was warm and wilted, and the coffee was sharp and rancid. I walked past the Purity girls and out into the night. One of them stared at me through the greasy window and made an exaggerated kissing face and waved, and I saw the others laugh.

I waited for a hole in the traffic to come along, then sauntered back to my noisy nest. I put the key in the door and opened it to smoke and light. Buckelberry sat on my bed. A stranger sat in the plastic chair.

"Make yourself right at home," I said.

"McGee, this is Mr. Yeoman."

There was going to be no handshaking. He held his glass up and said, "This we brought in, son. Exactly the same brand as yours. You got a nice taste in bourbon."

They seemed relaxed, watchful, reasonably friendly. I made myself a drink and took it over to the bed and sat beside Buckelberry. He had tucked his shirt in and wore a red-brown corduroy jacket with lots of pockets, all with flaps and buttons.

Jasper Yeoman was an astonishingly youthful fifty-eight. He had black hair combed back, just a little grey over his ears. He wore a dark business suit. He was a lean, long-limbed man. He had a long narrow brown face, deeply seam-ed, Indian-dark eyes, ears that stuck out far enough to give him a countrified look. He had horse teeth and a thin-lipped mouth with a small twisted and sardonic smile which looked habitual. He had great assurance, a steady stare, and he was the sort of man who would disconcert you by seeming to be amused by some joke you did not understand. He sat slouched with one limber leg hooked over the arm of the chair. They were waiting for me to make the move, and I damned well wasn't going to.

Finally Buckelberry sighed and said, "Jass here was curious about you, McGee."

"I can imagine he might be."

"Just to set your mind at rest," the Sheriff said, "we've got a pretty good line on that pair. The professor took off from home yesterday afternoon. His junk car is over to the Car-son Airport. The manifest says a Mr. and Mrs. Webber John-son caught the one-fifteen flight to El Paso this afternoon.

The ticket man says a big blonde woman and a great old tall skinny boy, both of them in big dark glasses."

"Near as we can find out," Yeoman said lazily, "Mona left the house about ten this morning. Two suitcases gone. Clothes and jewelry. The way it figures, you were at the Carson Airport to drive her car away for her. You could tuck it off in any one of those little roads off there behind Cotton Corners, after you'd taken it up to take a look around the cabin. There's only one thing makes any kind of damn fool sense to me. That's that Mona must figure she'd got one hell of a good hidey-hole planned out for her and the professor, and when we can't turn her up, we'll come back to paying more mind to that damn fool story of yours."

"What good would that do?" I asked.

"You look like a steady enough man," Yeoman said. "How come you sucked into this kind of foolishness? She convince you I stole her daddy's money and treat her cruel? Son, Mona has just come into her restless time, and the thing to do is just wait it out. She's gone romantic as a young girl. Let me tell you something. She isn't real steady. She like to tore herself up beyond fixing before I married her. She needs a firm rein. She needs a man half husband and half daddy to keep her settled down. She's got that poor professor in a condition where he don't know which leg to put in his pants first. Having a husband old as me, she's got a fool notion life is passing her by. If she'd been fertile it would have worked out better for her, I guess. But she hasn't wanted none for servicing, and until she got the romances, it seemed to please her just fine. She'll outlive me, and when I'm gone I'll leave things tied up so she can have an income that'll give her a chance to be a damn fool in every city of the wide world, if that's what she wants. But as of now I'm her husband, and I know better what's good for her than she does. I've whipped her when she was ripe for it, and it has settled her down nice and grateful for it. And I've bought her about every damn thing she set her mind on. I'm not begging and I'm not pleading. It's just that if you know where it is they plan to hole up, it'll save everybody a lot of trouble and nuisance. I'll even go this far, son. Once they're birddogged, I'll even hold off a week, ten days, before busting it up. Then she might settle down faster when she's back, having got herself at least some of what it is she thinks she's got to have."

"Now Jass," Buckelberry said in a very gentle voice.

"All right, Fred," Yeoman said. "I talk too much about private things." As I looked at Yeoman more carefully I realized he was drunk. I had not caught it before. He had the control of the practiced drinker—awareness of limitations and the automatic compensation therefore. He shook his head. "But God knows what crap she gets these goddam eastern friends of hers believing about me. That Weaver woman visiting, she looked at me the way I look at an old iguana. You'd think, for God's sake, I forced her into marriage." He unhooked his leg from the arm of the chair and leaned forward. "Mister McGee, her daddy and me raised us twenty years of pure hell, and he left her to me. I had no mind to marry anybody all my life. Nine years ago, when I hunted her down in Paris France she was the nearest thing to ruin you could see. She's a big girl, and she was down to a hundred pounds. She had the screaming fits, son. She didn't know where the hell she was. I'd let her stay loose too long, and when I thought of what Cube would think, it shamed me. I put her in good hands in Switzerland, and I hung around. They built her back up. Then what was I to do? Turn her loose again? She's fanciful. It wouldn't be long before a rough crowd would get hold of her again. So I did what made sense to me. I locked her up the best way I knew how, by marrying her and bringing her back here to her home place. And it worked out better for eight years than you could guess. She can fool you, boy. You look at her and you see a big kind of cool-looking woman, nice talking, sensible acting, and she can make you think day is night if she puts her mind to it. But she is still just a crazy kid underneath, with fool notions. And she's restless this year. I keep her anchored down to a good decent life. I'm too old, son, to be turned into a wild animal by the idea of her humpin' that professor. It saddens me some, and I resent it, but I can make a try at understanding it. And I am free to admit that when I get her back, I'll make steam rise off that cheating tail of hers, but it will ease her because she'll know she's been a naughty girl, and it is always easier on a person to pay for things than walk around with guilt. And it won't hurt my own pride any to get it out of my system. What you don't understand, and what she doesn't understand, is that, way down, she's dependent on me. I want to get her back before she runs herself into the ground again. Now suppose you tell us where they planned to go."

I did not know how to answer him. I knew he was clever,

but I could not believe he was so clever as to know she was dead, and be able to give such a convincing performance. I swirled the ice in my glass.

Fred Buckelberry said, "Were they going to get their permits and walk over to Juarez, and go down into Mexico from there? Or was that just a feint in the direction of Mexico? Were they going to fly west from there? California?"

I ignored him. I finished my drink and looked directly at Jasper Yeoman. I said, "I don't know a goddam thing about your marriage, Mr. Yeoman. I was standing next to your wife at two twenty-five this afternoon. Somebody hit her high in the back with a heavy slug at long range and she was dead before she hit the ground, face down."

For a moment the very dark eyes wavered and the mouth softened. Then he firmed up again. "I tried to talk man to man to you, son. I tried to get through. Let me tell you something. There is nobody in this wide world with any call to kill Mona. I would come the closest maybe, but it is the last thing I would ever do. You think you've got some obligation to stick to that fool story. You look like you had more sense. You irritate me, boy. I'm going to have Fred here run your ass right out of this county, and I don't want him being gentle about it."

I shrugged. "Fred is so impressed with being close to such a big taxpayer, Mr. Yeoman, he's forgetting what he knows about being a good cop."

"What the hell does that mean?" Yeoman said.

"I'm just an amateur. But I thought of wondering if that rock slide blocking the road was all accident. So I climbed up there and found that somebody had blasted that rock down. They wanted Mona to walk to the cabin. Why? I don't have any idea. If she had somebody with her, it gave somebody else a chance to run off with the car, so there would be a lot of time before it could be reported. They'd need time to clean up the area and lug the body away."

"He didn't say anything about that before, Jass," Buckelberry said.

"I can think of a lot of things a good cop would do," I said. "We were conspicuous in that little white car with the top down. Somebody would have had to see us and remember us between Carson and the cabin. And I think it wouldn't hurt to get a lab crew up to that cabin. I think that slug must have made a hole as big as your fist in her wishbone on the way out. All they would need is one little bit of blood or tissue that was overlooked." I stood up. "I get pretty goddam tired of this routine. I saw a woman killed. I knew her about two and a half hours. I didn't like her particularly. You can sit around and dream up your little fairy stories about where she is now, but she is damned well dead, and somebody wanted a lot of confusion about this, and I have the hunch John Webb is dead too. Was his old car checked for prints? You can chase me out of the county. I think it would be a favor. Because if I stay around here, I'll be sticking my nose in where it doesn't belong. Maybe that lab crew has a good polygraph operator. Why not check my story out? Hell, that would be too easy."

The fried-meat muscles bunched at the corners of Buckelberry's jaw. He had good control. He waited it out and looked at Yeoman and said, "I can do a little more checking, Jass."

"You do that."

"How about this fellow?"

Yeoman stood up and moved toward me and looked me up and down. "Hooo-eee," he said. "Now isn't he a big one. Fred, why don't you keep him around a spell?"

"Locked up?"

"Maybe he'll stay anyways."

"I plan to stay, Mr. Yeoman."

Without taking his eyes from me, Yeoman said, "Fred, pick up the jug and get on out to your car and wait there a minute. I want a word with you before I drive on home."

The Sheriff hesitated, picked up the bottle and left.

As the door closed, Yeoman said, "Sometimes I get the feeling the whole world is figuring out mean tricks to play on Jass Yeoman. You stand on top of the little hill, they can see you from all sides. Fast as you spin, your back has to be toward somebody. They could not care about her one way or another, but they could try to use her to gut me. Do you know what I'm talking about?"

"I think so."

"Give an old dog too many hot trails, he might just set and howl instead of moving out. You ever see one of those clowns that has all the dishes spinning on top of the sticks, and he has to run like hell, from one end of the line to the other, keeping them spinning?"

"Yes."

"I've got a lot of crockery up in the air right now, son.

Running back and forth so fast, anybody puts a stick between my legs, by the time I could scramble up there could be money spilled all over the place. And someone there to catch it. Some might even slop over onto Fred, just incidentally like."

"So?"

"I like a man first thing, or I don't like him and never will. I don't know where you stand. You look like you could turn mean as a sore-tooth snake. If you come up with anything you think worth selling to me, I'll buy it."

"Such as?"

"If you can't figure that out, you won't ever have anything worth selling."

He winked and ambled to the door, winked again and went out into the night. Drunk or sober, he was a man who would make sense as long as he was conscious. But he had lost me. He gave the impression of being aware of conspiracy. It had occurred to him I might be playing some more devious role in this matter, whatever it was.

I gave up. When I knew more, maybe I would understand it. So I went to bed. He still didn't believe his wife was dead. Somehow he gave the impression of not being able to afford that knowledge.

Though I tried to put it out of my mind, I fumbled at it as I slid toward sleep, like trying to untie knots while wearing mittens.

And I did like him better than I had liked his young wife.

three

I WALKED A MORNING-MILE into the middle of town and had breakfast at a convention hotel, The Sage, amid people wearing badges and bragging about their hangovers. There was a car-rental desk in the hotel lobby, and when the uniformed girl found I was not a guest of the hotel, she very carefully checked their dead-beat list of credit card numbers before, with manufactured joy, honoring mine. I wanted a cheap one, and while I was waiting for it to be brought around from the garage, I bought an area map at the newsstand.

The man brought a sand-colored Falcon around. I walked around it and found the deep dent in the back right fender. It was not noted on my sheet. I got the girl and we all stood and stared at it, and then she marked it on both copies of the sheet. One can never blame them for trying. The ones who bang them up run past the desk, toss the keys in, and go get on an airplane. I inspect cars I rent. I add up the tabs waiters hand me. I read the fine print on contracts. In these matters, I am a little old lady.

State Western University was in the town of Livingston, 44 miles due south of Esmerelda on State Road 100. There is an unreality about urban places in barren lands. I guess it is because the land was never put to any other use. It did not grow up where farms used to be. Three miles south of Esmerelda, its mere existence behind me seemed dubious and improbable. I drove through a land of rock and scrub, sand and brush, lizards and the sun-wink of unrusted beer cans. The huge flats of the broad valley had once been, I could imagine, the floor of some ancient lake. Esmerelda, according to the daily *Eagle*, had an unlimited supply of pure water from deep wells. This water accounted for its improbable location in the eerie silence of windy flats and sand-brown mountains.

Thirty miles of SR 100 were utterly flat, and then the

road began to climb and wind in long curves past hill slopes and harsh outcroppings of stone. Green patches were more frequent and evident. When I finally topped a ridge, I saw the town in the distance, perhaps a thousand feet higher than Esmerelda, and tucked against the flank of a long mountain that looked, in a trick of light, like a brown dog curled sleeping.

State Western was one of those new institutions they keep slapping up to take care of the increasing flood of kids. It was beyond the sleepy-looking town. Hundreds of cars winked in the mid-morning sun on huge parking lots. The university buildings were giant brown shoeboxes in random pattern over substantial acreage. It was ten o'clock and kids were hurrying on their long treks from building to building. Off to the right was the housing complex of dormitories, and a big garden apartment layout which I imagined housed faculty and administrative personnel. A sign at the entrance drive to the campus buildings read, No Student Cars. The blind sides of the big buildings held big bright murals made of ceramic tile, in a stodgy treatment of such verities as Industry, Freedom, Peace, etc.

The paths crisscrossed the baked earth. There were some tiny areas of green, lovingly nurtured, but it would be years before it all looked like the architect's rendering. The kids hustled to their ten-o'clocks, lithe and young, intent on their obscure purposes. Khakis and jeans, cottons and colors. Vague glances, empty as camera lenses, moved across me as I drove slowly by. I was on the other side of the fence of years. They could relate and react to adults with whom they had a forced personal contact. But strangers were as meaningless to them as were the rocks and scrubby trees. They were in the vivid tug and flex of life, and we were faded pictures on the corridor walls—drab, ended and slightly spooky. I noticed a goodly sprinkling of Latin blood among them, the tawny cushiony girls and the bullfighter boys. They all seemed to have an urgency about them, that strained harried trimester look. It would cram them through sooner, and feed them out into the corporations and the tract houses, breeding and hurrying, organized for all the time and money budgets, binary systems, recreation funds, taxi transports, group adjustments, tenure, constructive hobbies. They were being structured to life on the run, and by the time they would become what is now known as senior citizens, they could fit nicely into planned communities where recreation is scheduled on such a tight and competitive basis that they could continue to run, plan, organize, until, falling at last into silence, the grief-therapist would gather them in, rosy their cheeks, close the box and lower them to the only rest they had ever known.

It is all functional, of course. But it is like what we have done to chickens. Forced growth under optimum conditions, so that in eight weeks they are ready for the mechanical picker. The most forlorn and comical statements are the ones made by the grateful young who say Now I can be ready in two years and nine months to go out and earn a living rather than wasting four years in college.

Education is something which should be apart from the necessities of earning a living, not a tool therefor. It needs contemplation, fallow periods, the measured and guided study of the history of man's reiteration of the most agonizing question of all: Why? Today the good ones, the ones who want to ask why, find no one around with any interest in answering the question, so they drop out, because theirs is the type of mind which becomes monstrously bored at the trade-school concept. A devoted technician is seldom an educated man. He can be a useful man, a contented man, a busy man. But he has no more sense of the mystery and wonder and paradox of existence than does one of those chickens fattening itself for the mechanical plucking, freezing and packaging.

I found the administration building and parked and went in and stood at the main information desk and asked a gray-haired lady if I could speak to John Webb. It flustered her. She said he was an assistant professor in the Department of Humanities. Was that the John Webb I wanted to see? She was hoping it was some other John Webb. There was a student named John Webb. No relation. She struggled for the right phrase and finally said that Dr. Webb was absent from the college.

"For how long?"

"I am sorry. I do not have that information."

"Who can tell me when he'll be back?"

"I really couldn't say. Perhaps one of the other men in the department could help you."

"This is a personal matter."

"Oh. Then perhaps his sister . . . she might be able to tell you."

"Where do I find her?"

She thumbed a cardex, and said, "Hardee number three. The faculty residence buildings are in that direction, sir, opposite the large parking lot. You'll see the names on them. Hardee is the third one back."

I found it without difficulty. Each building was a complex of about ten or twelve individual residences, each with its own entrance, arranged so as to give maximum personal privacy, yet share a central utilities setup. They had used a lot of stone, adobe brick, walls, courts, covered walkways. I found the gate for number three, pushed it open, walked to the door ten feet from the gate. I could hear no bell inside, but as I was wondering whether to try knocking, the door opened and a young woman stared out at me. She wore what appeared to be a brown burlap shift, with three big wooden buttons that were not functional.

"Yes?"

"I am looking for Professor Webb. My name is McGee."

"I can tell you the same thing I told the other gentleman. And the same thing I have told the head of the department. I haven't the slightest idea where my brother is."

She had begun to close the door. I put my foot in the way. She looked down at it and said, "If you please."

"I do not please. I want to talk to you."

"There is absolutely nothing to talk about."

"What if things are not what they seem to be?"

"What do you mean?"

"What if he didn't run off with her? What if it's just supposed to look that way."

"What is your interest in this affair, Mr. McGee?"

"I am the only one who is absolutely certain Mona is not with your brother. Everybody else seems to believe it."

She waited a moment, and then opened the door. "Come in, then."

She led the way back to the living room. Draperies of a coarse and heavy fabric were drawn across the windows. She had evidently been working at a big mission table. Books and notebooks and file cards were in orderly array under a big bright gooseneck lamp. Music came from a big record player, turned low. It sounded like a small and irritable group of musicians who were trying to tune their instruments but couldn't decide who had the right key. She turned it off, went to the windows and yanked the blinds open to let the sunlight in. She came back to the table and turned the lamp off.

I watched the way she moved. She wore shabby deerskin moccasins. She moved lithely, with enough hip sway to pull alternating diagonal tensions in the burlap shift. Her arms and legs were very smooth and white and rounded, flexible with health. Her face was a long oval. The flesh around her dark eyes was deeply smudged. It made her look frail and unwell, but I suspected that was a normal condition of those eyes. There are eyes like that, the surrounding flesh permanently darkened. Her mouth was small and plump and without lipstick. Her nose was delicate. Her eyes had long dark lashes. Her hair was parted in the middle, dark and rather lifeless hair which was arranged in two curved wings across her forehead and drawn back and fastened in a loose bun. There was a large electric coffee maker on the mission table. "Coffee?" she said.

"Thank you. Black, please."

She went to the kitchen and came back with a clean cup and saucer, poured me a cup, and took hers over to the corner of a corduroy couch by the windows, and pulled her legs up under her, tucking the brief edge of the shift over white knees. I sat at the other end of the long couch, against the bright cushions.

"You contrived to intrigue me, Mr. McGee. Now you have the problem of continuing to do so. But I do not know your status in this."

"Mrs. Yeoman contacted me, through a friend. She thought I might be able to help her with a problem. I arrived yesterday noon from Florida. I talked with her about her problem. She wanted her husband to release her. She wanted money from him. She wanted to marry your brother."

"And you go about trying to make this sort of arrangement? Are you an attorney?"

"No. I didn't know what the problem was until I got here. And it didn't seem to be anything I would be interested in trying to handle."

"So she settled for half a loaf."

"No. Believe me, it was not her intention to take off with your brother, not unless it could be arranged . . . amiably. And financed."

"Mr. McGee, if you believed anything she said, you are as big a fool as my brother. And, believe me, he has proven himself a fool."

"By leaving?"

"He's finished here. You just can't do what he's done and expect to be taken back when the mad little adventure is over. If he was very popular here, and very political, he might have a chance of mending his fences. But John is neither. The unforgivable thing is that it is all . . . so obvious and vulgar."

"In what way?"

"Do you need an explanation? Gullible dreamy young professor meets oversexed wife of elderly rancher. Romance blooms. Actually, that's too tender a word for it. But it was his rationalization, of course. Real genuine love. That's what they have to call it, to keep some fragment of self-respect, I imagine. But it was and is just a nasty, ordinary compulsion of the flesh. John had never run into a woman like that before. Once she seduced him, he stopped having a rational thought. He was pathetic, believe me. Love? With that big obvious creature? How could a fine man love an animal? He was hypnotized by what was under her skirt. Excuse me for being coarse."

"These things happen."

She shrugged. "One expects them to happen, with women like that. But not with men like John. One doesn't expect a man like my brother to destroy himself for the sake of . . . access to a big meaty pretentious blonde floozy."

"Maybe he didn't."

"Mr. McGee, everything my brother dreamed of doing or being is dead. Maybe he can make a living in a correspondence school, or a textbook house, but his career is over. And he is a brilliant man. It's such a damnable waste. I couldn't make him see what an ass he was being. God knows I tried. We never fought like that before. He doesn't give a damn what he's done to me, either. Sacrifices I've made apparently mean nothing to him. Pride and devotion. They mean nothing. God, I've read about it enough times, how a sensual fixation can destroy a man, but I never thought it could happen to him. And it is all . . . so utterly meaningless. Some absurd little sexual spasms and releases, and the whole world thrown away just for that! I shall never, never understand it."

"Did you know he was going to run away with her?"

"I was afraid of it. He'd gotten so restless since the fall term started. Then, I would say about ten days ago, he changed. He seemed to be happy about something. He told me everything was going to work out. Arrangements

were being made. He seemed very smug. He'd set up his
schedule so that he had Tuesday and Thursday afternoons free
every week, and Monday afternoons free every other week.
He would leave on those afternoons and meet with her somewhere. And he would come dragging back here about seven
or eight at night, dazed and exhausted, wearing that foolish
grin. The damned woman was wearing him out with her de-
mands on him. He had the impertinence to suggest that once
things were all arranged, the three of us could live here.
Can you imagine her as a faculty wife? She is two years
older than John, you know. She would start telling the president of the university how to run things."

"Perhaps she told him that I was going to help her."

"Possibly. Oh, they were terribly optimistic about everything. They seemed to think that because they were in-
fatuated with each other, the whole world should find them
terribly attractive. But everyone knew it as . . . a distasteful
and unpleasant situation."

She got up and got the coffee pot, unplugged it and brought
it over and filled our cups. When she bent over mine I noticed she smelled like vanilla. I wondered if she had been
drinking it. It did not seem likely. This was one of the intense ones. She was perhaps four years younger than her
brother. I could imagine her plodding around NYU in black
stockings and short tweed skirts, arguing with a coffee-house
passion about abstract concepts, trying the painter-loft sex
and finding it overrated, trying the knock on the mescaline
and finding it made her sick instead of exalted, signing up
to picket this and that, sitting for hours of observation in
the UN, wearing barbaric jewelry designed by no-talent
friends, painting stage sets for amateur productions—all in
all an intense, humorless, intellectual child, full of heavy
dedications and looking for some shelf to put them on.

"Yesterday, Tuesday," I said, "Mrs. Yeoman picked me up
at the Carson Airport at noon. I understand that your brother
took off Monday afternoon. That seems a little previous."

"I imagine they had it all planned. I've been taking some
courses here. I have a Monday afternoon seminar. Mass Communication and Opinion Leadership. John had two classes
Monday morning. Contemporary Philosophy. And Philosophy in Literature. He had Monday afternoon off. I expected he would be with her. When he didn't get back by
nine o'clock, I felt uneasy. But I imagined he had somehow
arranged to spend a whole night with her. That seemed to

be about the summit of his ambitions lately. I thought he
would come in and clean up in the morning. He has a ten
o'clock on Tuesday. By nine Tuesday morning, I began to be
suspicious. I started looking around. His suitcase and some
clothing were gone, and his toilet articles. No note for me.
Not a word of explanation. He didn't even have the courtesy
to notify the head of the department. He just . . . left, like
a thief. As you probably know, he left the car at the Carson
Airport, and they flew from there to El Paso. I'll have to arrange to get the car, I guess. That's seventy miles from here,
northeast. All of this is very embarrassing to me. It puts
me in a very strange position. I had a long talk with Mr.
Knowdler, the Dean of Faculty. He was quite sympathetic toward me. This is the beginning of our third year here. I'll
have to give this place up, of course. But I can keep it until
November fifteenth, he said. John will come slinking back
before then, I imagine. It is just sort of a vacuum. I can't
make any plans. He'll need help. I don't know what will become of us."

"Do you work here too?"

"Oh, yes. Five mornings a week, in the communications lab.
Clerical work. But not today, because they are enlarging it
this week, tearing out partitions and doing a lot of new
wiring. I'm doing research here for one of the enrichment
programs. History of the Dramatic Arts." She looked wist-
ful. "It was a pretty good life here, Mr. McGee, until that
woman came into it, and upset everything. I didn't mind
keeping house for John. If he was alone, he would eat cold
things out of cans and his clothes would look like a va-
grant's. And he doesn't take good care of himself. He's
never been very strong. That woman won't take good care of
him. Why did she have to be attracted to him? Why couldn't
she have found herself some . . . truck driver or policeman,
some muscular cretin who could do a better job of giving
her what she so obviously wants?"

"Did you check to see what your brother took with him?"

"He packed and left. Evidently he took what he thought he
needed."

"If I ask you to do something which seems pointless, will
you do it?"

"Such as?"

"Would you check and see if he left anything behind
that he would logically have taken with him?"

"I don't think I know what you mean, Mr. McGee."

"Something which might be overlooked if somebody else did his packing for him. If it was supposed to look as if he packed and left."

"Isn't that a . . . a little melodramatic?" Her soft pale little mouth seemed to identify a bad taste. "A kidnapping?"

"If you don't mind looking."

"Not at all."

The sunlight was strong on the back of my hand. There were bright squares of fabric on the walls, primitive designs. I could hear the woman opening and closing drawers. Then there was a silence.

She appeared suddenly in the doorway, braced as if to dodge an imaginary blow. She held a small black case in her hand, about the size of a small book. She held it out toward me, and her mouth made little fish motions, and then she said, "He . . . He didn't . . ."

I took it from her and opened it. Two hypodermics. Spare needles. Test strips. Vials. Alcohol. I snapped it shut. "Diabetic?"

"Yes. Yes, he would *have* to have this with him! He has to inject insulin every morning. He is a *very* absentminded man, but he had to learn the hard way not to be careless about this. He learned by forgetting and going into diabetic coma. Or by giving himself too much and having insulin reaction. I can't imagine his forgetting . . ."

She sank into a chair. "But he could forget, of course. But he would have remembered this morning. It is so much a part of his routine. He has prescriptions. He could buy what he needs. Yes, that's what must have happened."

"Did anyone see him leave here?"

"What? I don't know. I don't imagine so. There aren't very many people here on Monday afternoons."

"Where was this kit kept?"

"In the bathroom medicine cabinet."

"He took his other toilet articles from there?"

"Yes. I . . . I see what you mean. It is . . . very strange. It makes me feel . . . scared." She frowned up at me. "You said it was supposed to look as if they'd gone away together. Why?"

"I don't know why." I saw her sudden change of expression. "What's wrong?"

"I don't know. I suddenly remembered something. Something he said last Sunday. We were having . . . one of those quarrels that didn't accomplish anything. I said some kind of snotty things about his having a big week coming up, with Monday, Tuesday and Thursday free for her. He said he would not see her Tuesday, yesterday. He said she would be busy. If he was planning to leave Monday . . ."

"He knew she would be busy with me."

"Then where did he go?"

"Where was he taken?"

"Please. Are you trying to make me more frightened?"

"What is your name?"

"Isobel. Isobel Webb."

I hooked a stool over with my foot and sat on it, close and facing her. "My name is Travis McGee, Isobel." I took her hand. After two yanks she stopped trying to pull it away, and sat uncomfortably rigid, looking past me rather than at me.

"Why are you acting so strangely?" she asked, wetting her mouth with a quick and pointed tongue-tip.

"I don't want to scare you. I'm going to take a chance on telling you something. Maybe I shouldn't. Maybe you'll fly apart. I don't want you to. I want you to hold on tight and ride with it. Will you try? Good. Now listen carefully. Mona Yeoman took me to an isolated cabin in the hills. At two twenty-five yesterday afternoon, standing just as close to me as you are right now, she was shot in the back and killed instantly with a high-powered rifle fired at long range. I walked out. When I came back with the Sheriff, her body was gone. All trace of her was gone. They will not believe me. They think I was trying to put up a smoke screen so she could make an easier getaway with your brother."

She searched my face. Her eyelashes were uncommonly long. "But . . . they got on an airplane yesterday. At one fifteen. They went to . . ."

"A big blonde woman and a very tall thin man, both in dark glasses, got on an airplane yesterday at one fifteen. I know damned well that Mona Yeoman was not on that airplane. At one fifteen she and I were in her little car heading for that cabin. We were practically there. The manifest gave the names as Mr. and Mrs. Webber Johnson. John Webb. It was like wearing a sandwich sign. If he was trying to escape notice, would he have picked a name like that? Was he that stupid?"

"No. You . . . you use the past tense."

"Was he planning to meet her Monday afternoon?"

"N-No. He had too much work piled up. He was going to

come back here and work. He had papers to grade. They were on that table when I got back here. I've turned all the class materials over to the department. Other men are taking over his courses, until they can find someone."

I was watching her closely. She seemed very jumpy, but she seemed to be holding on pretty well.

"I *know* Mona is dead, Isobel. And there seems to be a lot of organization behind this. Substitutes took that flight. I know Mona is dead, and the only way the plan could be made to work, to look as if they ran off together, would be to kill your brother too."

She closed her eyes and her hand clamped hard on mine. A small smooth pale hand, but quite strong. When she opened her eyes, they looked blank and dazed.

"But it is so . . . so strange! What would be gained?"

"We don't know. Not yet. But the search would continue, looking for a pair of lovers in hiding, and after a while it would die down. I guess the traditional guess would be that they had made a new life for themselves somewhere else."

"Would her husband do that?"

"I don't think so."

She looked at the black case. I had put it on the table beside the chair. "Then that is sort of evidence, isn't it?" She stirred as though to stand. "I should tell the police."

"Now wait a minute, Isobel."

"Why should I wait a minute? If he was . . ."

"Somebody went to a lot of trouble to make it look as if they'd run away."

"Then why was she killed where you could see it happen?"

"I don't know. Maybe they didn't have any choice. Maybe they had it planned another way, and it didn't work out and they had to improvise."

"But if my brother was abducted . . ."

"Prove it."

"He left his kit here."

"An oversight. He picked up another at a drugstore in El Paso."

"But . . ."

"Livingston is in Esmerelda County. Sheriff Fred Buckelberry is conducting the investigation."

"He and a deputy were here last evening. At about eight o'clock. They told me about the car and the flight they took. Mostly it was to tell me to get in touch with him right away if I got any word from John. They were . . . lazy and ironic and sarcastic about the whole situation." She tilted her head to the side, frowning. "It does seem more logical."

"What do you mean?"

"I didn't really think he would . . . ever actually run off with her. I thought he had too much balance for that. I was just trying to make him see that he had to stop seeing that woman. There was too much gossip about it. I couldn't imagine his arbitrarily destroying himself. But if people came here and . . . took him away. . . . He hated violence. He . . . wasn't a strong man. He never wanted to . . . to hurt anyone. . . ."

Past tense. I think she suddenly realized she was using the past tense. Her eyes filled and she made a small yowl of heartsick pain and hitched forward in the chair, and slumped against me in the helpless awkward abandon of pain and sorrow. I held her. She rolled her head back and forth against my chest, gulping and whimpering, automatically seeking that small comfort to be had from a physical closeness, even with a stranger.

But suddenly when I patted her shoulder, she tensed and jumped back away from me as if I had been a basket of snakes. "Excuse me," she said in a narrow little voice. She seemed to make herself small in the chair. I saw then that her eyes were a very very dark blue, the darkest blue I have ever seen in eyes of man or woman. Lifeless hair, pliant white body, smell of vanilla, and sexual fear. Noble refuge for the unrealized woman—caring for the adored brother. I realized that she had been uncommonly bitter about the Mona-brother relationship, alluding to the sexual basis of it the way she might discuss a suppurating wound. No wonder she had thought these were two fine years. Her twenty-fifth and twenty-sixth? A good place to wait away the nubile years, hasten the drying of juices, all in the honorable name of dedication. A Mona Yeoman would be repulsive to her, inevitably. Mona walked with too much awareness of her body and its uses.

"You met Mona?" I asked.

"He thought we should get along. That was one of his worst ideas. She patronized me, as if I were some backward child. I just . . . I just can't imagine her dead. She was so . . . blatantly alive, Mr. McGee."

"Travis. Or Trav."

"I am not very good at first names. It takes me a long time."

"It's a gimmick I don't particularly care for. I thought it might make you feel more at ease with me, Isobel."

"I'm almost never at ease with people. I . . . I guess it was the way we were brought up."

"How was that?"

"Both my parents were artists. My father was successful and my mother had an inherited income. We lived miles from anyone. The school lessons came by mail. They took turns teaching us. Canada in the summer. A little island in the Bahamas in the winter. John was the one who was always ill. We all fretted about him. I was always so healthy. You learn to . . . invent games you can play by yourself. They died three years ago. Just two months apart. They were very close. We always felt like outsiders, John and I. And that made us close. And now . . . What am I going to do! What in God's name am I going to do!"

She got out of the chair and edged past me and walked to the table. She picked a book up and dropped it and turned, leaning against the table. "Why would anyone want to kill him? I can't believe you. You know that, don't you? I just can't believe you."

"About Mona?"

"Y-Yes, I can believe that. She was so . . . definite. She could make enemies. But John is such a mild man, really. With a wry little sense of fun."

"How in the world did they meet?"

"They met just about a year ago. Her husband came to a dinner party at the president's home. We were invited. Mr. Yeoman had given some money to a scholarship fund. John was seated next to Mrs. Yeoman. She pretended to have some interest in contemporary philosophy. They were talking Heidegger, Broad, Ryle, Sartre, Camus. She was one of those clever people who know just what to say about something they know nothing about. And she had met Camus in Paris years ago. John is at his best when the conversation is in his field. He can say very challenging things. She started driving down every week to audit his Friday seminar in the Philosophy of Democracy, paid avid attention, kept a very detailed notebook, did a lot of outside reading. That's the way it started. It was a vicious smokescreen of course, all that manufactured interest. He was just a new species to her. I told him to be very careful. She didn't seem to be in any great hurry. She didn't seduce him until last April. He came blundering in with some fantastic story about her car break-

ing down. She used to come right here to pick him up.
Shamelessly. It was really pathetic. He didn't stand a
chance, of course. She was a very clever and determined
woman. And bored, I expect."

"Do you have anyone to stay with you, Isobel? Or anyone you can stay with?"

"No. I don't need anything like that."

"I don't think you should phone that Sheriff."

"Because it doesn't mean enough that his kit should be
here?"

"Partly that. But this whole thing has been . . . organized
pretty well. I want to find out as much as I can. Quietly. I
think that if I start making any noise, I could end up working on the county roads. Whatever happened to Mona and
your brother, it is one factor in something else. There are a
lot of things stirring around under the surface."

"But what if my brother needs help!"

She was close to the edge again. "Isobel, the only way we
can force action to get help to him is to prove that they did
not take that plane yesterday. People are too damned willing to believe they did, even her husband. I think the Sheriff
may be a little opportunistic, but I don't think he's corrupt.
I'm pressuring him to look further into my story of Mona's
death. If he comes up with something, then it should be evident that neither of them took that feeder flight."

"But how long will that take you! He could be in some . . ."

I saw that I wasn't going to be able to quiet her down. I
would have to move her around. "I want to go back to the
Carson Airport. I want to poke around a little. You have to
get that car, don't you? Why don't you come along?"

She hesitated and gave an abrupt nod. "Give me time to
change."

four

BEFORE SHE LOCKED the house, I had her show me where the car was kept. The carport was in the rear, off the kitchen. The side road passed in back of all the garden apartment layouts. The side walls of the carport were high. If somebody had waited for John Webb, or had entered after he was at home on Monday afternoon, it would have been no trick to pack him up, bundle him out and drive away with him. I did not mention to her that they could have hammered the top of his head in before even putting him into the car. And in this vast empty chopped-up terrain, there were thousands of quiet places to put him.

She locked the place, after checking to be certain she had her set of car keys. She had changed to a gray skirt in a loose weave. It looked a little too big for her. She wore a yellow cotton blouse, and brought a sweater along. She had an old lady purse, dark gray leather, well worn and very sedate. She wore nylons and black shiny moccasins. And she wore big wraparound sun glasses, tinted almost black. With her eyes obscured, her face seemed totally without expression, and smaller than before.

She directed me down into the village and told me where to turn. She sat erect and remote, purse in her lap, hands folded over the clasp. Violence leaves such vulnerable victims.

"Where in the Bahamas?"

"What? Oh, I don't think you'd know it. It was just about a mile long and about three hundred yards wide. It was near Old Mallet Cay."

"South of the Joulters. On the banks, a little way in from the Tongue of the Ocean. It's very tricky water there. Plenty of coral heads."

"Then you do know it!" Her voice sounded younger.

"If it's the one I'm thinking of there's an old gray house there, pretty well storm-battered, near a nice little protected

52

anchorage. Most of the island is volcanic rock. The house faces west."

"That's it!"

"Did you sell it?"

"We never owned it. My father got it on a lease from the crown. Ninety-nine years. You can't sell those leases, you know. They can be passed along to the direct heirs, and when the time is up they revert. John and I have talked about going back one day."

"Was there no inheritance?"

"Mother's money was just for her lifetime. And it wasn't a big income, really. My father was always in total confusion about taxes. And he made fantastic investments. After everything was settled, John and I got a little over nine hundred dollars apiece. You know, I loved that island. There's a beach and a bar behind it. I can remember how lovely it was in the moonlight. The beach was like snow. We all used to get as brown as Bahamians."

"You don't look as if you'd ever been in the sun."

"I think I got too much of it when I was a child. My lips are allergic now. They puff up and break out in sores. I'd love nothing better than to just . . . lay in the sun and bake until the world gets far away."

"How long since you've tried?"

"Years."

"They have some new things now. You know, miracles of chemistry. There's a paste that screens out every kind of ray."

"Really?"

"Guaranteed."

"Could you get me some? Would you know what to ask for?"

"Of course."

"This may sound . . . perfectly idiotic to you. But . . . if you are right . . . if some horrible thing has happened to John, it would be easier for me to bear it if I could just bake myself all loose and weak and far away. It's like a drug for me. Mr. McGee, when did you last see that house?"

"Two years ago, in the spring."

"Did you go ashore?"

"No. But I put the glasses on it. It's all shuttered. It looks sound."

"I guess it would be a great deal of work to make it livable again, clean out the drains and cisterns and all that. We had a sturdy old boat, a dear thing. Four hours to New

Providence, and that was the great event, picking the wind and weather, leaving when it was just bright enough to see."

Her voice was lighter and more flexible when she talked of that, her posture more relaxed. I made note of it. It could make her easier to quiet down, knowing that much about her.

I took the long tilted curves of the mountain country, working up, and then through a pass and down the far side to a plateau country, to fenced areas where there was a coarse gray-green grass, to open land of mesquite, sagebrush, cactus. This was State Road 202, less traveled than 100, a little narrower and older. There were a few towns built in the Spanish pattern. The road curved around them, avoiding the old route of narrow cobbled streets constricted by walls, and on the newer road were the cafes and garages, small pastures of automobiles most brutally slain.

As we neared Carson I could see, far beyond it, the mountains I remembered from the flight in, purpled with distance, streaked with high marks of canyon snow. The airport was on the north side of town. The terminal was new and small, pale fabricated stone and tinted glass panels. There was free parking in lots on either side of the building. A quarter mile away was a shabby sun-weathered hangar and private service area, where a score of small bright planes were staked out in formal array on the dusty hardpan. There were about forty cars parked in the two lots. A little cream and red plane was shooting landings.

We arrived at quarter after noon. "I don't see our car," she said.

"What is it?"

"It's a dark red DeSoto. I don't know what year. It's quite old. No, it isn't here anywhere. But the Sheriff said it would be here. I wonder if John could have . . ."

"Let's see what we can find out," I said, and parked. We walked out of sun heat into the airconditioned chill of the terminal. A man stood just inside the door. He had a chauffeur hat, a big belly, a damp cigar end, little gray pebbles for eyes, and an air of petty authority.

I started to walk by him, and then stopped and went back and said, "Pardon me. I was supposed to pick up a car off the lot out there, an old maroon DeSoto. It was left there yesterday or the day before. Would you know anything about it?"

He looked me over and moved the cigar to the other corner of his mouth. "It was took off, mister."

"What do you mean?"

"What I said. They put a hook on it and took it off. Maybe about ten this morning. It was a city rig, so I'd guess it went down to the car pound, like they do for parking wrong, or a recovery of something stole."

It bothered her. She had more questions than I could answer. I took a dime into a pay booth while she stared at me through the glass, her mouth tight, her eyes invisible behind the dark lenses. The city police switchboard passed me along to one man who transferred the call to another man, who said that the county had requested they pick up the car and hold it. "I'd say it was a case they want to check it over," he said, "because the way the request came through, it was to keep our hands off it, so we sent a man along with the city wrecker to put it in gear and so on without messing up anything they maybe are looking for. It ain't been checked out yet, and you got any questions about releasing it, what you do is check with the Sheriff's department."

I folded the door back and left the booth and told Isobel.

"What does it mean?" she asked. "Why would they do that?"

"Maybe they're willing to admit there could be two versions of what happened. In front of Yeoman last night, this was one of the things I said the Sheriff should be doing. So he's doing it. But it's a way out chance. Fingerprints work fine on television. But, on a rough guess, they get a usable print off one out of every hundred guns, one out of every twenty cars. A man adjusts the rear view mirror by hand, he can leave a good imprint on the back of the mirror, if the surface is smooth enough. Sometimes a thumb print on the front of the glove compartment. It is usually more meaningful to find a car wiped clean, steering wheel and door handles. No smudged prints and broken prints. Then that has some significance."

She peered up at me, dark head tilted. "It's some kind of a strange logic, isn't it? If he didn't go off with her, and you say he couldn't have, then there would be no point in his bringing the car here."

"Let's get some lunch."

There was a lunch counter in a corner of the terminal. After we had ordered, I left her there on the stool and went and looked at the boards. Westways had the one fifteen to El Paso, with intermediate stops. The flight originated three more stops north. It was due through again today.

At close range the ticket man was too old for his butch-cut.

"On your flight two oh three, would that be the same flight crew as yesterday?"

"I wouldn't know. Why?"

"Could it be?"

"I guess it could be. The rotation system is too complicated for me to follow."

"Will the flight crew come into the terminal?"

"It's just five minutes here. They're on time. They should be in at ten after one."

I went back to my cooling hamburg. I told her what I had in mind. I told her I wished I'd asked her for a picture of her brother. She took a billfold from her gray purse. She took a color snapshot from a compartment in it. She and her brother were standing squinting and smiling in the sunlight, with one of the campus buildings behind them. He wore a pale suit and his necktie was crooked. She said the picture was over a year old. John Webb was tall, narrow, pallid, hollow-chested. He had an untidy shock of black hair. His smile was pleasant. He did not look like the sort of man Mona would have been interested in. He looked vague and anxious to please. But you can never tell. Maybe, after Cube and Jass, she'd had her fill of forceful males.

The two-engine plane came in a few minutes early. There were three or four to get off, three or four to get on. They wheeled the steps up to the door forward of the wing. I followed the passengers up. The smiling stewardess held out her hand for my ticket. The smile was habitual. The uniform was navy blue and pink. She was a taffy blonde, a little too hefty for her skirt, her lip dewed with the sudden perspiration of the heat at ground level.

"I'm not a passenger," I said. "I just wondered if you had this flight yesterday."

"Yes sir?"

I showed her the picture. "Do you remember this man? Tall and dark and thin. He was with a sizeable blonde. They both wore sun glasses. They got on here and went to the end of the line."

"Yes, I remember that couple."

"This was the man?"

"I don't know. I thought the man looked . . . tougher than this man somehow. I remember them because I had . . . well, not trouble, really. We had a light load. They had a bottle.

We're not supposed to permit that. But you know how it is. There was an old lady in front of them. She complained to me. She said they were talking dirty. I moved her to another seat. They weren't being particularly loud." She looked at her watch.

"Do you remember how they were dressed? Or anything else in particular about them?"

"She wore a pale blue seersucker suit and red sandals with high heels, and she had a big red purse. That's where the bottle was. I don't remember about him. Dark slacks and a light jacket, I think. He had a long stringy neck and some little scars here, below his ear. Let me see, they were on the port side, so they would be on the right side of his neck. Those operations they do for glands. Sir, I'm sorry but I have to . . ."

"Thank you very much. What's your name?"

"Houser. Madeline Houser."

I went back down the steps. They were pulled away, the door dogged tight. As I walked back to the terminal, they turned to taxi and the air blast pressed against my back, hurrying me along, kicking up spirals of dust and gum wrappers.

Isobel was waiting inside the door. I took her over to the lounge chairs facing the tinted glass and the runways and sat beside her and told her what I had learned from Madeline.

She shook her head sadly, her mouth puckering. "It wasn't John. Nothing fits. No scars on his neck. He wouldn't talk that way. Where is he? What happened to him? Will you tell the police what that stewardess said?"

"Let me keep this picture for a while."

"Certainly. Should I report John as missing? Won't that stir something up?"

"We should be more certain just what we're going to stir up."

She hit the arm of the chair with her fist. "Why are you so hesitant? Certainly this is a police matter now. Maybe I should phone the newspapers. Damn it, we can't just *sit* here!"

"It's better than rushing off in all directions."

"He could be tied up somewhere, all alone, sick."

"So if you start all the sirens screaming, Isobel, anybody who knows anything about it is going to dig a hole and crawl in and wait it out. We need to know more. We need to get some small idea of who did it, who would benefit, why it was done. All this wasn't just an impulse. It has to make some kind of sense. I want to talk to the lawyer she retained. He's from outside the county. Belasco. But I don't know his name."

"I know his name. Wait a moment. I'll remember it. I heard John mention it when he talked to Mona on the phone. It begins with an M. An Italian name. Mazzari. Yes, that's it."

"Where's Belasco?"

"Not too far from here. Another twenty miles east, I think."

We drove into Belasco at twenty after two. It looked half the size of Esmerelda, and had the look of having been there a lot longer. It had plazas and defunct fountains, Moorish arches and mission churches, a big riverbed with a tiny stream in the bottom of it, fall tourists with cameras, a spectacular view of the Candelero Range. Rogan and Mazzari had offices in an old yellow bank building on the central plaza. The girl said that Mr. Michael Mazzari was over at the courthouse and would I care to make an appointment. The courthouse was within walking distance. The corridors were hot, damp and dingy. We found Mazzari in shirt sleeves by a corridor drinking fountain, talking with two other men. The attendant spoke to him and pointed us out. He nodded and in a little while he came over. He was a dark bull-necked little man with a quick white toothy smile. He was just beginning to thin out on top. He appraised Isobel from ankles to the part in her hair with that utter frankness of the confirmed and practiced hunter.

His handshake was hard. "McGee? And Miss Webb. Oh? Miss Webb? John your brother? I see. Or maybe I don't see. My girl tell you where to find me?"

"I told her it's an emergency."

"Is it?"

"It certainly is," Isobel said forcefully.

He excused himself and went over and spoke to the attendant outside the courtroom doors, then took us to a small room nearby, evidently one of the witness rooms, a putty-colored cube with golden oak furniture. We sat at a scarred table and he said, "It's a civil action in there. Automobile accident. I hate the goddam things. The jury is off trying to figure out how much to give my client. I may be able to spare five minutes or two hours, depending how they get along together. What's the emergency? I assume it has something to do with Mona Yeoman."

"She was murdered yesterday afternoon," I said.

He had the look of a man hard to jolt, and that jolted him. Astonishment gave way to suspicion. "Now wait a minute," he said. "Even old Jass couldn't put the lid on anything like that. And I haven't heard a thing."

"It was supposed to look as if she'd run off with John Webb. There's no body. Webb is gone too. A pair of reasonable facsimiles took a plane out of Carson yesterday."

"Maybe it was Mona and John Webb."

Isobel started to object. I hushed her and told Mazzari the facts—the long-range shot that slammed her down, the insulin kit, the stewardess's observations, the police pickup of Webb's car.

He whistled softly. "What a wild situation! Look, without you on the scene, Mr. McGee, it would have worked. Excuse the rude joke, Miss, but those two laid the groundwork for running off together. They had the hots. That's what made her restless enough to bring me into it, on the money end."

"Was there any truth in her claim that Jasper Yeoman robbed her?"

He stared at me. "Who am I retained by?"

"Not Mona. She's dead."

"Where do you fit into this, Mr. McGee?"

"You couldn't solve her problem by legal means without taking too much time. And even then it was dubious. She thought I could find some shortcuts. She paid my way out here. But I didn't like the sound of it."

"So now I represent you?"

"Either of us who needs it. Provided you . . . you aren't in the wrong pocket."

He looked irritated. "I don't mind the question. I am not in anybody's pocket. I could be richer than I am, believe me. I wouldn't be screwing around with this kind of negligence suit. I am one independent wop, and pretty fierce about it, if that's what you want. You could be further ahead hiring somebody with clout in this area. Mona came to me because I've got the maverick reputation. I spit in the eye of the mighty. I'll never get elected to public office, thank God."

"So now we have a lawyer. First question, Mr. Mazzari . . ."

"Mike."

"I'm Travis. This is Isobel. Mike, did Jass bleed that estate?"

"Bleed is not the word. He took it out of her pocket and put it in his. But it would take two years and a staff of accountants to nail it down. It wasn't at all crude or obvious. It was a case of making very plausible but unwise deals on unloading the asset values in the estate, unloading them through dummy setups and eventually picking them up again very cheaply for his own account. With careful management, that estate could have been worth five million by today. But it petered out to nothing some years back."

"How about the courts?"

"I don't think you'd ever turn up any evidence of corruption. Jass was a good old boy. He could take you dove hunting. Or quail hunting. Everybody knew that little girl would never lack for a thing. When he puts his attention on it, he can charm birds down out of the trees. He's known to be very sharp, but honest. Perhaps he told himself he was simplifying, just putting all the marbles where he could watch them better, getting rid of legal restrictions which could cramp his style. Also, this culture has a feudal flavor about it. The wife is the vassal. A flighty woman who could put her hands on her own money might be hard to handle. Forcing it into the courts would be tough. It could be done, with a lot of time and a lot of money. There would be reluctance. Why make a stink when things are fine the way they are? You understand. The fact remains, he gave that estate one damned complete ransacking."

"He was in trouble?"

"Oh, he was in bad trouble. He had to dip into something, and the estate was handy. He had a lot of things going sour all at the same time. Oil, cattle, plastics, trucking line, little airline. His wells pumped salt water, and his cattle froze, and he got into litigation on a processing license on the plastics operation. Union troubles with the trucking line, and three fast crashes on the airline. His money was fading like snow in a heavy rain."

"Was he a lone wolf in all those operations?"

"No. A lawyer worked closely with him. He's dead now. Tom Claymount. A very shifty character. And there is the man who was, and is, Jass Yeoman's partner in a lot of ventures. Wally Rupert. It is pretty obvious that Wally would have had to know where Jass was getting the money to bail them out."

"Mike, here is the jackpot question. With all you know about the financial fast-dealing that went on, what would be the effect of Mona's death, if it was known? If she rolled her car, for example."

"Interesting. Let me see now. Internal Revenue would have that file twenty years old. You have to assume they would be on their toes, eager to take another clip at the Fox estate. She was the sole heir. They could move in with some very awkward questions. Where did it all go, fellows? We can assume they would be a sore trial to Jass Yeoman. They have the manpower to do the digging, and they are not as tolerant as the local court would be. Assuming the estate merely held its own, they would be after several hundred thousand dollars. What happened to the estate? Even with the rubber stamp of local court approval, Jass could find that question very embarrassing."

"All right, what if she disappeared forever?"

"Without a trace? That would hold the feds off for seven years. Then they would take the necessary action to have her declared dead, so they could reach for their share of the estate that isn't there any more."

"Somebody wants her to disappear. Jass?"

"I wouldn't think so. I don't know. It doesn't seem likely. Not the way it's being done. He is ruthless, but not in that way."

"Could anybody hate her enough to want to kill her? Could she have had somebody else on the string?"

He shook his head. "That doesn't seem likely. Hard to think of her dead. There wasn't much malice in that woman. She looked like a complete woman, but she was emotionally immature. She got dreamy about John Webb, like a young girl. It was a lovely romance."

Isobel snatched her glasses off and said, "How can you say that! She was a cheap, vulgar, vicious sexpot."

Mazzari looked at her with mild astonishment. "Are we talking about the same gal?"

"Maybe she could fool you and fool my brother, but she didn't deceive me. I can tell you that. She was in heat. That was her problem."

"Isobel, honey," he said gently. "He is your big brother and the only family you have. So naturally you guard the manger. But, believe me, Mona was just a lovesick kid. Jass understood that. And Jass understood that sooner or later she'd get over it, and when she did, she would want things the way they were before, the nice daddy-figure to watch over everything, position in the community. He knew she couldn't work out anything permanent with your brother. They're both dreamers. And both pretty nice people, actually, with cases of delayed adolescence. Jass could be more tolerant because he is, after all, twenty-six years older than she was. She was sincere. She wanted her freedom. She wanted some of her money. She wanted to marry your brother."

"All she wanted was to sleep with him!"

"Which is a very natural byproduct of romantic love, honey."

"Stop calling me honey!"

"I'll put it this way to you, Miss Webb. If you can't comprehend it, stop knocking it."

"What is that supposed to mean?"

His grin was lazy and charming. "People who censor books are usually illiterate."

She understood instantly and perfectly. She tried to leave in anger, but it looked a little too much like flight. She banged the door shut.

"I lose more clients," Mazzari said.

"She'll be all right."

"It was a sneak punch. I wouldn't needle a man about being deaf or blind. She looks choice, but by the time you made it, she would be too old to enjoy it. A lifetime project. Too bad. It doesn't make it any easier for her to face up to her brother being dead. If you haven't been waltzing me around with these other items, he very probably is."

"I know."

"And your Miss Webb isn't going to take it very well. Neurotics and sexual cripples never do."

"I think she's letting herself begin to admit it, an inch at a time. She might be able to take it pretty well. Everybody is an amateur psychologist. Great devotion to the brother. With how much resentment mixed in? But it isn't my problem. None of this is my problem. I should go back where I came from."

"But this made you angry?"

"Yes. It made me angry. And those clowns thought I was making it up. Can you brief me on that Buckelberry?"

"Fred is all right. College athlete. Honor student. A very pretty and very ambitious wife. Two kids. Graduate work in police methods and procedures. But he doesn't want to be Sheriff too much longer."

"Political bug?"

"No. There's a lot of money in Esmerelda County. He's rubbed up against a lot of it. He handles himself well. And he has got the executive touch. He'll do his job, but he isn't going to offend any of that money over there that might be important to his future. He's looking."

"Do you think Jass Yeoman could be behind this whole thing, Mike? After all, hiring you, trying to hire me, she *was* trying to damage him."

"How seriously? She was playing pretend. She had the scene of herself standing up in court, pointing to Jass, denouncing him, riding off into the sunset with a million dollars in hand and loverboy professor beside her. When I was trying to unravel her problems, I used to get the play by play. She would just chew the living hell out of Jass, tear her hair, break things, scream at him. He would ride along with it, and a few days later they would go out to his old ranch and ride and swim, kidding around, playing gin for blood, checking out the riding stock he was breeding out there, and he would jolly her right into bed. She would be so damned mad at herself when she'd come back to town, and swear it wouldn't happen again, and actually make herself forget it had happened. Mona believed what she wanted to believe but, you see, Jass was her reality. Daddy, friend and lover. And the rest of it was just some game she was trying to play. Jass knew it wouldn't last. But it made him itchy having to wait it out. He could have chased John Webb a thousand miles, but that would just martyr him and make him more attractive to Mona. I think, if she'd proposed it, Jass would have settled for giving Webb a month or two of her. But Mona and Webb idealized their love. They called it forever. An arrangement like that would have cheapened it. Jass didn't want to lose her—both for his own sake and for hers. Maybe he didn't have the right intentions when he married her nine years ago. But it worked into something else, as it often does when the marriage is for other reasons. She talked a lot to me. I saw just how it was. If she had had it in her power to smash Jass she would have done so, because that was part of the daydream, but she would have been heartbroken later."

"And would she have brought anybody else down with Jass?"

"If she could have done anything?" He shrugged. "Claymount is dead. The old judge is dead. It could have stung

Wally Rupert a little, maybe, because any real thorough checking would show he was in on that grab."

The attendant rapped on the door and opened it. "Coming back in," he said.

."Thanks, Harry. Travis, if you want me along when you talk to Buckelberry, if you want to talk to him again, it can be arranged."

"Thanks, I'll manage."

"Stay in touch," he said and hastened off, shouldering himself into his suit coat.

five

I FOUND ISOBEL standing by a drinking fountain, close to the wall but not leaning against it, her chin up, dark glasses on.

I took a drink and straightened up and wiped my mouth and said, "I like that feisty little man."

"You damn bastard!" she said. "She paid your way to come here. What were you talking about in there, you damn bastard? Were you eulogizing that whore?"

"Isobel, dear, you shouldn't try to swear. You don't do it well. You make me think of a little girl in her Sunday frock, trying to throw mud balls."

"Don't be quaint. I had about all the sappy sentimentality I could stand in there. Mazzari is a dirty-mouthed little man. You came here to try to work Mrs. Yeoman for some money, didn't you? She's dead now. I think I understand why you're so reluctant to stir things up about my brother being missing. It would spoil your chance to chisel money out of whoever did it. Did you and Mazzari figure out some nice safe blackmail scheme?"

"If you'd stayed we'd have had to cut you in, Isobel."

She stamped her foot. "I *insist* that we take some official action immediately!"

"Well, if you will start walking, we'll get into my car and we'll go to Esmerelda, and we will tell our tale to Sheriff Fred Buckelberry, if that isn't rushing it too much."

"But . . . I thought you . . ."

"Come along, dear Miss Webb. And learn a few more facts of life."

"Oh, you *know* so damned much about everything, don't you?"

We arrived at the Sheriff's wing of the Esmerelda County Courthouse at five after five. The Sheriff was not in. The desk man said he was expected very shortly. We sat on a corridor bench to await him. He came in about five minutes later, walking swiftly, followed by a meek looking young man in dark glasses and a pale blue denim suit. When Buckelberry saw us, he stopped so abruptly the other man nearly piled into him. "McGee," the Sheriff said. "Miss Webb." He gave a furtive glance up and down the corridor and said, "Come on in."

We followed him back through overcrowded office space to a corner office. A man tried to spring at him with a sheaf of papers but Buckelberry waved him back. He ushered us in and closed the office door. He had a blue rug, blue draperies, white walls, gray steel furniture.

He went to his desk, pressed an intercom switch and said, "No interruptions." He released it and said, "Miss Isobel Webb. Mr. Travis McGee. Lieutenant Tompkins. He is with the central CID setup for this area. Sit down, please. I imagine you have something to tell me or ask me, or you wouldn't be here. I will tell you something first. It may save us some time. We've just come from the hospital. The pathology lab. The search crew up at the cabin this afternoon found a dried fragment of tissue stuck against the side of a stone about seven feet from where you said she fell, McGee. The pathologist identified it as lung tissue. Mrs. Yeoman's blood type was on file at the hospital. We have a match there. In addition, the Webb vehicle was left in the airport parking lot between midnight and two A.M., Monday night. I got a phoned report from the technicians Lieutenant Tompkins sent to Carson to check the car over. It had been wiped clean. No significant stains. They vacuumed it, but I imagine that report won't mean much when we get it."

He gave me a long challenging look, and I knew I was not going to get any apology or any thanks.

I turned the other cheek by saying, "Nice work, Sheriff. I'll give you what we have very briefly. John Webb was a diabetic. He left his insulin kit behind. It was kept in the same cabinet with his toilet articles. They were taken. I talked with the stewardess who had the same flight yesterday. The couple who took that flight drank and used bad language. The male had noticeable scars on the right side of his neck. John Webb had no such scars. They were a rough match for Mrs. Yeoman and Mr. Webb. The woman wore a pale blue seersucker suit, red sandals with high heels and carried a red purse. The man may have been wearing dark slacks and a light sports jacket. The name of the stewardess is Madeline Houser. I am certain you can get an official statement from her."

"You are inclined to meddle, McGee."

"Meddle!" Isobel gasped.

"Sheriff, I drove Miss Webb over there to get the car. You told her where it was. It was gone. We had lunch. I realized that same flight was due. I thought that the best thing to do would be to try the stewardess while it was still fresh in her mind, if it was the same one. If you didn't get to her for three or four days, I doubt she would have remembered much about it, certainly not the details of how the woman was dressed. It was an impulse, Sheriff."

Tompkins cleared his throat and said hesitantly, "I suppose that any information . . . regardless of source . . ."

"I want to know where my brother is!" Isobel said loudly.

"So would I," Buckelberry said.

"Aren't you going to look for him?" she demanded.

He dropped his curt official manner. He had proved his point. He was a good cop. Even if I had pressured him into it, through Jass Yeoman, he was still a good cop.

"Miss Webb, be logical now. He left or was taken away Monday afternoon. This is Wednesday. Today you've decided he didn't go away with Mona Yeoman. All day yesterday you were sure he had. Miss Webb, my God, there are better than six thousand seven hundred and fifty square miles in Esmerelda County, and this time of year every last stinking little dirt road is passable. Every decedent we got on hand is identified, and there's no John Doe in any hospital. I signed away my soul to get the use of a helicopter all day to try to locate Mrs. Yeoman's little white car, and there's no word on it yet. I'm working a hundred-man county with a sixty-man outfit. Now just exactly what the hell do you expect me to do?"

She seemed to crouch and aim at him. "Sheriff, I expect you to spread the word. I want this on television and radio and in the newspapers. I want everybody to know that Mona is dead and my brother is missing. I want a posse and . . . and boy scouts and . . . the National Guard searching every darned inch of all those square miles."

He leaned back and made a tent of strong hairy fingers and stared at her. "You force me to be frank with you, Miss Webb."

"Please do. It would be refreshing."

"I'm convinced there's been a murder. I haven't a damned thing to go on. I haven't even got a body. I won't bore you with what I have to do. Coroner's jury, completed file approved by the state's attorney, grand jury indictment. Miss Webb, my cop sense tells me that the very best thing I can do is continue a quiet investigation and let whoever did it believe they got away with it, that we believe Mrs. Yeoman and your brother took off for El Paso. If we start beating all the drums, this thing is going to get so muddied up we'll *never* get anyplace. And the people we want will hide twice as hard."

"Then my brother's safety means nothing compared to your performance."

"My cop sense tells me your brother is already dead. Alive he could turn into a very awkward loose end. I think he died before the woman died."

She shrank in the chair and put the back of her hand against her mouth and stared at him. "Even if there was only one chance in a thousand . . . You can't stop me from going to the newspaper."

"Go ahead, Miss Webb. They'll check with me. That would be automatic. I'll tell them that Mrs. Yeoman and your brother took off together. That's the same thing I'm going to tell Jass Yeoman within the hour, that I checked it and it was just the way we thought it was. You can stir up a little gossip, Miss Webb, but you can't give them anything they'll print."

"But if Mr. McGee comes with me and verifies it."

Buckelberry glanced at me and said, "Ask him."

She turned and looked at me. I shook my head sadly.

"You damn bastard," she whispered.

"Isobel, dear, these are the facts of life I was telling you about. I think I know what Sheriff Buckelberry is going to do next. Listen to him."

"I am going to comb this county for tall dark thin men with scars on the right side of their neck, Miss Webb. And for buxom blondes who own blue seersucker suits and red shoes. And I am going to let some things slide I will catch hell for later, and I am going to check out those people, and I am going to find one or both of them. And I am going to make them sweat and beg for the chance to tell me every little thing they know. If I did it your way, they might never come back into this county. And I would rather have either of them than ten thousand cross-country boy scouts. I am going to be checking out every heavy scope rifle in the area. I am going to send two damn good Indians into those rocks tomorrow, up north of that cabin. I am getting an expert analysis of the explosive used to block that road, and I'm going to find out where it came from."

"Where is my brother!" she yelled.

He sighed, opened a steel file drawer in his desk, poured a jolt of bourbon into a glass and brought it to her.

"I don't drink."

"For God's sake, girl, this is not a cocktail party. This is medication. Gulp it down!"

She took it, shot a sidelong and unfriendly glance at me, drank it down. She gasped and coughed.

"What can I do?" I asked the Sheriff.

"Try to settle her down."

"Aside from that?"

"Aside from that, stay out of this."

"Why aren't you telling Jass?"

"Because I'd get no help from a crazy man, any more'n I can get from a keyed-up woman."

Isobel thrust her arms out, fists balled. She screwed her face up and yelled, "FIND MY BROTHER!"

"Oh dear God," Buckelberry said. Without a hat his head looked strange. There was so much wide jaw, it made his head look triangular, almost pointed at the top. "What am I going to do?" He looked as if he wanted to put his head down on his desk and cry.

I tried a different approach. "You can't reason with her, Sheriff," I said. "This one is a genuine intellectual. She is an emotional basket case. She had an unhealthy symbiotic relationship with the brother. She's about twenty-six and so she's supposed to be grown up. But you can see for yourself. Childish frenzy. Limited contact with reality. She is so basically screwed up, a thing like this is going to land her at the funny-farm sooner or later, so the simplest thing is get it over with right now. You are authorized to commit, aren't you? The lieutenant and I are witnesses to violent and irrational behavior. Frankly, Sheriff, I would feel safer if you would kindly stash her away. Somebody thinks this elopement gimmick worked in spite of my seeing her killed. And if it gets out that it didn't work, they might want to correct mistakes, and maybe leaving me alive was one of them. So if she could be tucked away and given some nice sleepy pills, it might be the best thing for everybody, her brother included."

He saw my wink. She couldn't. He said, "Sometimes you make enough sense to astonish me, McGee. Miss Webb, you'll get the best of care out at Piñon Springs."

For a few moments I thought we had pushed it too far. Her head swiveled in fast erratic motions as she stared in turn at the three of us, a glint of actual madness in those strange blue eyes. She clamped her hands hard onto the arms of her chair and sat, eyes closed, chin on her chest. She took very deep and audible breaths, her round breasts lifting against the yellow fabric of her blouse. Then her breathing softened and her hands loosened. She seemed to lift her head with an effort. She looked at Buckelberry and said in a quiet and controlled tone, "It is only natural that I should be very concerned about my brother."

"I understand that, Miss."

"Obviously you know more about this sort of thing than I do, Sheriff. I present one fact for your consideration. The Yeoman woman is dead. Nothing can be done for her. We do not know that my brother is dead. I think that should be your priority. He was taken from our home. Kidnapping is a federal offense."

"We have no proof he was taken. Merely a supposition."

"If you will give me your word that you will make finding my brother your first consideration, I will promise to . . . control myself."

"You have my word."

She grasped her purse and stood up slowly, timidly, looking as if she was poised to run. "Now if Mr. McGee could take me home?"

"If we have any news, we'll contact you at once, Miss."

I went out with her. She stumbled against me, walked uncertainly toward the corridor door, then stopped and leaned against the wall, head down, eyes closed, breathing deeply again.

"It's all right now," I said.

With eyes still closed she said, "I suppose it is all in getting used to knowing that you are nothing."

"I beg your pardon?"

"It's too cruel, you know, to look directly at things." She looked solemnly up at me. "Then you know that your father was glib and tricky and second-rate, and you know your mother was a very silly woman, and you know that your brother was really not a very good teacher, not much of a man, not much of anything. And you know that you are wasting yourself, running from a thousand things, hiding away at a third-rate institution in a damned wasteland. So why should the Sheriff or anybody care, one way or another? The illusions are so much easier to live with, Travis. The golden parents, the noble brother, the high calling, the devotion. The mysterious princess with the wise sad smile. Oh Christ, Travis, if you live without illusion, what do you have?"

"Come along, Isobel."

I took her arm and steered her toward the door. "What do they want of me?" she asked. I knew that They wasn't the police. Parents, perhaps. Or an amalgam of parents and brother and all the people of the world who had said, "My, what a bright strange little girl!"

I took her through the late brass of sunlight and across the open square to where my rental car was parked in a street narrow as an alley, in a deep black of shade. I put her in, and when I went around and got behind the wheel, I realized she was shaking all over. I had the impression that if she unclamped her jaw, her teeth would chatter.

"Isobel?"

She wrenched around to face me, her mouth stretched into ugliness. "And what the hell do you know of relationships? Symbiotic! Limited contact with reality! How could you even pretend to recognize the intellectual position? Oh, you have your lousy little vanity, Mr. McGee. You have a shrewd quick mind, and little tag ends of wry attitudes, and a sort of deliberate irony, served up as if you were holding it on a tray. And you have the nerve to patronize me! You have all your snappy little answers to everything, but when they ask the wrong questions, you always have fists or kicking or fake superior laughter. You are a physical man, and in the best sense of being a man, you are not one tenth the man my brother was." Her eyes went wide and dazed. "Was," she repeated softly. She had sunk the barb herself, and chunked it deep, and she writhed on it.

She huddled into her misery, face against her knees, grinding out the little rusty sobs. I pulled at her and gathered her in, against automatic resistance. I got her face tucked into the hollow of throat and shoulder, a hand pressed against the nape of her neck, an arm around the supple arch of her back. She clung. She was a foundering boat in a terrible sea. But she was still clamping down on the sobs, her back knotting. I was encouraging her. It was like getting a sick gagging child to vomit. "Come on. Let go. Let it go, dear."

It was cool in the deep shade. She squeezed at grief, miserly, choking at it. I could feel a terrible tension building in her, rising, and then it broke at last, in a great yawning loosened yaffling animal sob. All the wires had broken, and she could lose herself in it, throwing herself into each spasm, all softened and steaming and hopeless, freed for a time from that terrible prison of the highly complex personality wherein they are condemned always to observe themselves as though standing a bit to one side, watching themselves. A clot of young boys came down the alley, stared, sniggered, guffawed, made obscene gestures and went on. She settled into a dull rhythm, and after a long time that began to die. With the slow persistence of the sick or the very drunk she began to push herself away from me, to sort herself out, dogged and weary.

She sat apart from me. She was a mess. Her face was bloated, marked with angry patches of red. She got tissues from her purse. Every few moments a dry sob would shake her like a monstrous hiccup. The neat wings of hair were matted and in disarray. She looked closer to thirty-six than twenty-six. She looked at herself in her mirror, and with a slow and clumsy effort she fixed her hair. From time to time she sighed very deeply. She had made a sodden mare's nest of my shoulder.

Watching her I was reminded of the way a fighter will get up—one of the good ones. He lands face down in a way that means he can't make it. But at the count of three he begins to move. He pushes the canvas away. He comes up onto one knee. At nine and a half he is up, tottering and drifting and dreaming, perhaps grinning foolishly, but he is up and moving and his pride brings his gloves up, and he can take a huge frail slow swing at the opponent charging in to knock him down again.

She straightened humbled shoulders and said, "I . . . I guess there are some uses for the physical man."

It was that kind of gallantry based on an iron pride.

"The traditional handy shoulder."

Her glance was swift and sidelong. "Thank you for the shoulder." She took the dark glasses from her purse and put them on. "Now I feel shy and funny."

"To have been seen in that condition? Want one of my snappy comments, on a tray?"

She tried to smile. "Please don't. Why am I so exhausted?"

"You used yourself up. Want some coffee? Food? Drink?"

"I want to be home in my bed."

The square was in shadow. By the time I left the city the sun was gone behind the hills to the west, and the dusk land was blue. Her head kept drooping, and she would give little starts as she woke up. Finally she sagged over against the door on her side, head awkwardly cocked, hands loose in her lap, palms up, fingers curled.

She awoke when I stopped in front of Hardee Three, but she was as dazed as a trip-worn child. I walked her to the door. She said she would be all right. I said I would phone. She nodded absently. I took the key from her fumbling hand and unlocked the door for her. She turned and said, "Good night."

I patted her shoulder. "Get a good sleep."

She nodded and stood tall for a moment and kissed the corner of my mouth, a child's automatic kiss, the unconsidered gesture. I do not believe she was at all aware of having done it. She trudged in, turned on a light and closed the door. I guessed that she would be in bed and asleep in ten minutes. It was a little after eight. Twelve hours' sleep would be the best thing that could happen to her.

Strange little button. Comforted by being held. Great reservoirs of affection. But blocked in every other direction.

I pushed the little car on the way back to Esmerelda. The people at the Latigo Motel were nervous about their money. They were reassured to find out I now had a car. It comforted them. I showered and shaved and changed and went down to The Sage for two huge broiled lamb chops in their Sundowner Grille. A tipsy woman in a paper hat blundered by my table and chided me severely for not wearing my badge. I promised I would do better next time.

six

THE SOUTHWEST SECTION of the city was the old part, now the center of the Mexican-American community. The far newer and most desirable residential section was to the northwest where there was some contour to the land. I arrived at the Yeoman place at ten thirty. It was in a fold of the land, lushly irrigated, high enough so that when I got out of the car on the broad slick expanse of asphalt drive, I could look out across all the lights to the city in the clear cold night air. The house was low and huge, and something that bloomed in the night had an aromatic fragrance. Most of the house was dark. As I started toward the front a side door opened and Jass Yeoman said, "McGee? Come on in this way, boy."

I crossed a small terrace and he let me into a comfortable study. A man's room. Leather and wood, stone and books and bar, cluttered desk, gun rack, logs chuckling comfortably in a big deep fireplace. He had a glass in his hand. He told me to fix myself a drink. The expanse of wall behind the bar was dominated by a huge oil portrait of Mona Fox Yeoman. She wore a deep shiny blue, cut low. She sat on a bench and looked out at the room, wearing a small and knowing smile—a woman four or five years younger than the one I had seen die.

Jass wore slippers, a gray flannel shirt, khakis faded almost white. I sat in the leather chair opposite his. He said, "Every Wednesday night of my life I'm down at the Cottonwood Club. Steak dinner and poker. Dealer's choice, but it's usually shotgun. Three cards down and bet, get one more down and bet, one more down and bet, then play it like draw poker from there on out. You play poker?"

"Yes. And shotgun. It runs rough."

"That Wednesday game is worth about three thousand a year to me." He pointed a thumb over his shoulder. "Cook and the maid and the houseman and the gardener are

74

back there in quarters now, gabbling about it. El Patron is home on a Wednesday night. Or maybe they don't give a damn. Who knows?"

"Are we playing poker now, Mr. Yeoman?"

He studied me. I wondered at the blood heritage. Some Indian I guessed. Way back. I had not noticed his hands before. Thick hands, big-knuckled, with heavy veins. Hard labor, long ago. Nothing else will do it.

"What makes you think you know the rules?" he asked.

"I don't. I'm guessing at them. Things have a different flavor out here. Power is centralized in a different way. It's a feudal system. It goes against my grain, but I have the hunch that the solitary knight in his tin armor would take one hell of a thrashing. So I have to sign up, or I can't play. But I don't know how much cover I get."

"It isn't all as simple as it used to be."

"Nothing is."

"This solitary knight you brang up, boy. He rides in and picks a castle and signs up. You could be picking one with a busted moat and the towers falling down, and everybody out to lunch."

"So the knight is the type who can't stay on the horse and he's scared of dragons. Maybe it's the best deal he can make."

"You think I made an offer last night?"

"Didn't you?"

"You wouldn't have come around unless you had something."

"Mr. Yeoman, if I give you a card and you play it wrong, I could be . . ."

"For chrissake, McGee, you're signed on! Anybody moves against you, the whole castle gets dropped on them."

I leaned back, turning the glass in my hand. "She wanted to hire me to pry her loose from you, based on half of what I could pressure you to settle on her. She heard about me from a mutual friend. I know you plundered her estate. I know she was your ward. I think I know why you thought it smart business to marry her. I also have the feeling it worked out a lot better than you counted on."

"You're in a funny line of work, McGee."

"I'm a salvage expert. But I didn't want this job."

"Why not?"

"Just a feeling I had about her, that actually she was hoping there was nothing I could do. But she felt ob-

ligated to go through the motions. I think she was setting
herself up for the tragic renunciation scene, Jass. Tears,
goodbye to the lover, trudge home to the husband. I have
the feeling that's what she wanted next. To moon around
here until you were sufficiently impressed with her broken
heart, and then settle down. Where she belonged. You look
skeptical. Ask Mike Mazzari. He sensed that it was just a
romantic game. I think the game was about over, for her
at least. But they gave her no time to prove it."

"They?"

"The ones Buckelberry is looking for. They didn't clean
up the area perfectly, Jass. The lab crew found proof today.
A fleck of lung tissue and the right blood type. The ones
who took the plane were standins. Webb is probably dead
too."

He leaned his head back against the high back of the chair
and looked as if he had gone to sleep. A log slipped into a
new position, and sparks went up. He finished his drink and
got up slowly. He went and stood with his hands jammed
into his hip pockets, looking at her picture.

"You know what kind of water we're pumping from those
deep wells, son?"

"What?"

"Fossil water, sweet to the taste, laid down in the times
when this was swamp and lakes and giant lizards, ferns like
trees. We take it and when it's gone it's gone. Tomorrow all
them pumps could give one big gassy belch and suck nothing
but stale deep air. And this whole county would die."

"I didn't know that."

"They know it. They don't think about it. It scares the
piss out of them to think about it. It's like a man never
thinking he has to die. But the end is there. For this county,
and for any man in it. They herd new folks in here and
drill more wells and suck it away faster."

"It seems stupid."

He turned to the bar, replenished his drink and came
slowly back to the chair. "Hell, it *is* stupid." He wiped his
face, forehead to chin, in a slow gesture. "Waste. Hope. I
don't know. You take a quick look, there you are with
the world by the balls. Look again a minute later and you're
an old fart thinking of the ten thousand ways you had it
and blew it, every time. One day it turns out to be too
much trouble. That's all. Just too much goddam trouble. You
see, boy, I knew it last night. Forty years of poker. I saw it

in your eyes. I saw the way it put the hooks into your mouth and changed your mouth. Freddy Buckelberry, for the love of Christ! I got his call tonight. Jass, boy, everything is like we thought. Yup. She took off with the professor, sure enough. What the silly son of a bitch doesn't know is that last night was the night. Not tonight. I was a little stoned last night. And I shall get a little stoned tonight, son. Last night I took the Chrysler out, way over onto the mesa road. It was a political son of a bitch, from nowhere to nowhere, and I got me a piece of the state money when they put it through. Cold moonlight up there, son, and forty miles of it like an arrow. It was moving up close to a hundred when I turned the lights off, and it went up one hell of a way from there, until that big car was a very tender little dancing thing. Hit a big bull jackrabbit. Hit him on the rise with a crack like a shot and he kept going right up. Damndest thing you ever saw. He was blood and bone too. Maybe his clan saw him go, and they'll have legends about him. I took my foot off, banged it into neutral, took that long coast back on down, stopped by a runty tree. I set for a time, got out and looked at the front end, rabbit-size welt on top of the curve there, deep, with blood drying there and some hair caught in the edge. I fingered that hair, pale stuff and soft. I walked over by the runty tree and pissed into the sand and stood and looked at the stars. I told myself there would be times I would draw to four hearts and ease the hand open and see that fifth one. I told myself there would be the brandy and the cigar after the good steak, that feeling of ease. I told myself I was still the old he-coon, and I'd have that big warm swing of a knowing woman under me, that time when you know it's near and nothing in creation is going to be able to stop either one of you. I whistled pieces of tunes and worked the car around and drove back, slow as an old lady, lights on. Long after I thought I would have passed that rabbit I came up on him and stopped with the lights on him, and I got out for some fool reason I will never know. I had exploded him pretty good, but there was clean fur on him, solid meat on him. I felt him and he was warm still. I picked him up and crossed the ditch and got down on my knees and dug like a dog does, dug him a deep hole and put him in and covered him over with my handkerchief before I filled it in. Like, for God's sake, a kid with a dead bird. I patted the dirt down, and still on my knees I looked up at the stars and asked them what kind of damn fool they were making of me. I knew it wasn't any good, boy. Poker and brandy, cigars and fresh clean tail. No good."

He finished the drink, took both our glasses back to the bar and made fresh. I knew it was no time to say anything.

He handed me my drink and sat down. "Know what I keep remembering the most about her?" His grin made him look younger. "Three years ago. I was in the market for some brood mares and took her on up to Montana with me to look some over. There was good spring grass and flowers where we were. We walked up a hill and down the other side. I liked the mares. She didn't like the man selling them. My God, we'd start jawing at each other about any small thing sometimes. There wasn't a soul within two miles of us. The horses were grazing back by a brook. We were in that green bowl of grass and flowers. And there we were, nose to nose, yelling at each other. Suddenly she gave me a crack with her open hand that spun me halfway around. Usually I could guess about when it was coming, but she fooled me that time. I had a sore tooth and it hurt like hell. I gave her back a good one that turned her eyes empty for a half a second. She collected herself and swang again and I took it. I swear to God we must have whammed each other six times, and I saw her mouth twitching just about the same time I was beginning to see how funny it was. Then we were howling with laughter at each other, crying with it, like kids. And just about ninety seconds later we had both pair of riding britches off and we were nested down into that sweet grass and flowers like teenagers. Now isn't that the damndest thing to keep remembering?" He chuckled. "We both puffed up on the side of the face like ground squirrels taking a nut home."

He went over and poked the fire up. "Love? What the hell is love, son? I married her because I was nervous about stripping her estate. She married me because she was drowning and I came within reach. This professor thing, I felt exasperated the way you do when you see any good friend being a damn fool about something. She brang that lawyer over from Belasco, and after he snuffed around, he knew it would be uphill all the way, and a damned long trip. She sicked an investigator onto me, and I told the chief of police, and they taught that fellow local manners. Then she got you, whatever the hell you are. Salvage expert?"

"I'm a high-level Robin Hood. I steal from thieves."

"That wouldn't be a crowded occupation."

"Jass, isn't it pretty damned plain that the shot was really fired at you?"

He heaved up out of the chair and went over to a mounted pair of bull horns. They were on a long plaque that swiveled at one end. He turned them up out of the way. I caught a glimpse of the cylindrical wall safe before he stepped in front of it. I heard the chunking sound when he closed it and spun the dial. He came back to the chair. Without warning he flipped the stack of money at my face. I got my arm up. It bounced off onto the floor. It was paper-taped fifties, with the $5000 imprint, and the initials of whoever had counted it.

"Let's not fake what kind of interest you've got in this thing, McGee. Now you're saved the trouble of trying to con me."

I pushed myself up out of the chair just far enough to aim the kick. I kicked the money at the fire. I was trying to kick it in. It fell short. But it fell close. "Don't try to tell me what I'm interested in, Jass."

The top bills had begun to curl and change color. A first little wisp of smoke rose from them.

"You've got an interesting way of bargaining, boy."

"Throw me a more important stack, Mr. Yeoman, and I'll aim a little better next time."

"Money don't mean a goddam thing to you, eh?"

"I am very fond of it. I'm a little particular about the way it's offered."

We sat in silence. I couldn't read his face or those Indian eyes. The corner of the top bill blackened and a little necklace of red sparks began to eat a semicircular hole into it.

"My God, you're a stiff-necked son of a bitch, McGee."

"I said that according to local ground rules, apparently I have to join up somewhere. I didn't say I was for sale."

After a long time he got up and shuffled over to the hearth. He picked up the money by the cool end and slapped the sparks out against his pants, leaving a black smudge. He walked over to me. "I've got your name right? Travis?"

"Trav, usually."

He placed the money carefully on the leather arm of the chair. "Trav, if you'd like to help out a little, I'd be pleased to have you. Kindly accept this little token of my affection and esteem. If I was twenty years younger, we'd go on out into the side yard and bloody each other up for about forty minutes. That's the only way to get to be friends with a son of a bitch like you."

He went back to his chair and picked his glass up.

I put the money into the inside pocket of my jacket after slipping the charred bill out. I tore the charred corner off it and put the bill in my wallet. As though there had been no interruption, I told him all I knew about it thus far. I ended by saying, "Buckelberry didn't tell you because he thought you'd turn into a crazy man."

"Was it a sane man buried that bull jack under an Irish linen handkerchief?"

"Sane in a sense she might have understood, Jass."

"If I go crazy it is going to be from wondering who did it and why."

"She told me she was aware of being followed lately. She thought you were responsible."

"Me? Hell no!"

"Two men questioned her maid about her, the one who quit to get married."

"Dolores. Dolores Canario. Let me see. It's something else now. Estobar. Mrs. Juan Estobar. What the hell would they be after Dolores for?"

"Questions about your wife's personal finances. Dolores and your wife wondered if you were trying to find out if she had squirreled enough away to run away on."

"Son, that is a question I would never have to ask. I learned not to let her have any charge accounts. She got her fifteen hundred personal money the first of every month, and there wasn't a thing she had to use it for, and she was broke by the fifteenth regular."

"So somebody questioned Dolores."

"It sounds to me like a tax investigation, asking that kind of question. When they are working up a case against you on a balance sheet basis, they have to figure what you spend to live. Understand?"

"Not very well. I'm sorry."

"Trav, suppose you were worth a hundred thousand dollars ten years ago. Suppose today you're worth six hundred thousand. Suppose, every year, your net after taxes was fifty thousand. Suppose it cost you thirty thousand to live. Okay, your net worth should be three hundred thousand, not six hundred thousand. So they can build the case and come at you and say that you had three hundred thousand in income you didn't report. Fraud. There's no statute of limitations on that, boy. They can go back to 1913, the year the act was passed. God damn it, I thought I was in perpetual audit and all clean. But it sounds like they're whipping up a little surprise for me. And it can be a surprise, son. They can spend two years working up their case, and you get two months preparing a defense. You know. Funny thing."

"What?"

"I'm trying to get steamed up and I can't. I should go right over to that phone and call Charlie Baker and roust him out and have him check his contacts and find out what they're up to. But I can't seem to give that much of a damn. A tax mess right now would raise hell with a lot of things. But I can't get myself agitated."

"Jass, could they develop a case on that basis?"

He gave me a long slow smile. "They sure as hell could, son. I've been half expecting it for years."

"Could it be based, in whole or in part, on your taking over that estate?"

"Son, the way I picked up the money Cube left scattered here and there, I couldn't exactly declare it as income, could I?"

"Mazzari told me today that she was in such a romantic condition, she would have hurt you if she could, and been damned sorry later."

He started to ask me what I meant and then realized what I meant. "By God, if they'd got around to sitting her down and taking a statement, and she'd given them that big detailed gripe about what happened to this and to that her dear daddy left her, I would have been in the sorry-sling for sure."

"Don't misunderstand me, but doesn't that give you a motive?"

He looked at me in a way which made me glad I would never have the job of quieting him down—twenty years ago —or now. He had the look of the long hard bones, the meat tight against them, laid on in the long flat webs of hard muscle, ancient meat of the western rider, sunbaked, fibrous and durable. He had made trouble in a lot of far places and settled it his way, or he wouldn't have lasted. Cube Fox and Jass Yeoman must have been quite a pair.

"I am misunderstanding you too damn fast," he said in a deadly whisper.

"So fast you're not thinking clearly. If it would give you a motive, it would give somebody else a motive, somebody whose welfare is very closely tied to yours, somebody who would go down if they topple you, Jass."

I saw him work at the anger, pushing it back and down, tucking it away. He frowned. "I go it pretty much alone, son."

"You said you were like that clown with all the dishes spinning on the end of sticks."

"Right about now. Yes. Because I've been unloading things. You want to sell something, you have to pretty it up some. You have to throw money into it to make it look smart and peppy. Like you take an old house, you want to sell it good, you put in a new kitchen to knock the breath out of a woman so she can't even hear her husband talking about dry rot in the sills. In about four ventures I've been digging deep into working capital to fancy them up. I figured to come out of it in a year maybe, with just the horse ranch which damn near pays out by itself, and this house, and about a six or seven million liquid condition which would give me a borrowing power of that plus five times that amount, and I had it in mind to put all them eggs into one basket by taking over control of a very nice little company which I don't even whisper out loud to myself, son. They've got basic patents in about five different areas of the mining industry, and about twenty million cash reserve and nothing but a short-term debt structure. I'm getting too slow for all the wheeling and dealing and I figured to get me my own personal mint. I've got some bright boys working on all the angles of it, but nobody has a piece of the action."

"Okay. When we talk about power, we talk about power vacuums too. Who runs things around here? Beside you?"

"I guess it would be the boys around the Wednesday poker table at the Cottonwood Club. Boone Kendrick, Joe Gay, Tom O'Dell, Fish Ellery, Jaimie DeVrees, Paul Tower. And maybe two that don't play. Wally Rupert and Sonny Madero. Between us we got the whole ball of wax, mining, banks, newspaper, radio and television, cattle, real estate, transportation, construction, housing, power and light. A couple hundred others fight for the scraps left over. I am fixing to stick some of those boys with the items I want to unload."

"Mazzari said Rupert was a partner of yours."

He raised one eyebrow. "Son, it's not that close. He still

has small pieces of two things, and when I get those peddled, we'll be finally unlatched."

"But it was a lot closer than that?"

"Lord yes! We were in there, sweating and scratching, shoulder to shoulder for a long time." He gave a mirthless laugh. "We used up half our working time watching each other. We got hooked up together out of desperation, you might say. And when we got well, it was a delicate chore getting unhooked without getting gutted. We're both loners."

"Jass, all I can do is talk off the top of my head. Sometimes an outsider can see things in a different way. You can tell me if this question is nonsense. If Mona had given a detailed statement to the Internal Revenue people, and if you were indicted for fraud on that balance sheet basis you talked about, would you have to prove that the stolen money went into joint ventures you and Rupert were operating in order to keep from taking the whole rap?"

He stared at me. He knocked the drink off and got up and moved slowly to the bar. He started to fix his drink, turned and stared at me. "Not Wally, son. Not him. Get that out of your head."

"Jass, if they are slowly building up a case, would it be logical for them to contact Wally Rupert?"

"I don't know. They might. They might not."

"If they did contact him, he would get the idea they were after you, and he should let you know, shouldn't he?"

"By God, he would!"

"You talked about Charlie somebody, with good contacts. What if Charlie found out Rupert had been contacted, interviewed, and had said nothing to you? Would that mean anything, Jass?"

He finished fixing the drink. "He would be anxious to cover himself. Christ, we've got it all buried pretty damned well. It was years ago. A lot of the poeple involved have died off. Some of it was pretty raw, but what could they prove?"

"Raw?"

He sat down, looking uncomfortable. "As executor, I'd sell a hunk of Cube's land to the XYZ Corporation for fifty thousand. XYZ would be Wally and me, but not on the records. XYZ would hold it and resell it to ABC later on for forty-five thousand. That would still be Wally and me. Then we'd sell it to somebody who was really hot after it. We'd sell it for say fifty thousand again, having sort of established that price on it, and take fifty thousand over the table, and a hundred thousand underneath."

"How much did it all amount to, Jass?"

"Understand, son, I was scrambling for my life, and so was Wally. We'd made it from nothing, and we were set to lose it all because we didn't have the cash to protect ourselves."

"How much was involved?"

He waited so long I didn't think he was going to answer. "Call it a million four, boy. I came out with about seven eight hundred thousand. Wally got maybe four hundred. The rest went for expenses and a little gift money here and there, where it was needed. But you understand we didn't see it right off. We had to use it to bail with to keep from sinking, and it didn't really come back to us until we were over the hump. You know, we could have thrown all that in and still gone broke. But once things paid off all right, then we had that much extra."

"Could Mona have made any statement about Rupert being in on it?"

"She could have got it from Mazzari. There's a bright boy. Mona, one time when we were screaming at each other a couple months back, seemed to mention something about Rupert and me being a pair of thieves. I needed Rupert. All by myself I couldn't have put up enough smoke screen. But he had so many things going for him, we could shove papers around until sometimes even we couldn't figure out how we'd worked it. I want to tell you one thing, Trav."

"Yes?"

"I played it close and I played it sharp. But that is the one and only damn time in my life I stole. I plain had no other choice. The money was there. And I knew that if Cube knew the whole thing, he would have said go ahead, because he would have known I'd never let Mona want for a thing, no matter what."

He smiled. It was half grimace. "But I know damned well I've got to call Charlie Baker, just to prove we're wasting our time wondering about Wally." He stood up. "Come look at my new phone gadget."

I went to the desk with him. There was an important-looking box affixed to the phone, constructed as a part of it. He fingered through a small file, picked out a plastic card, shoved it into a slot and pressed a button. The phone briskly dialed a ten-digit number.

When the operator inquired, he gave her his number. He gave me a shark grin. "They make it impossible for a man to call a friend long distance, then they lease you a gadget makes it almost as easy as it used to be. Fix a drink and go on over and set, boy."

He had one of those special mouthpieces on the phone which made it impossible for anyone in the room to hear his end of the conversation. He talked for about five minutes. He came back and said, "Charlie'll find out. He likes to make it sound impossible. That's so it'll look as if he's earning his money. When he gives me the facts, he'll sound as if he risked his whole career to do me a favor."

"What's Wally Rupert like?"

"He's sixty now. You talk about feudal. Now there is one feudal son of a bitch, believe me. He don't have five friends in the world, but he's sure God got enough family to make up for it. He's gone deep into the service industries these past few years. Dealerships, laundries, hotels and motels, shopping centers. And the old bull-boar has been breeding his own labor supply. His old spread, eleven miles north of here, it's got so many houses on it now they call it Rupertville. He married young. Married Helen Holmes and had six kids by her. When she died, he married her kid sister, Catherine. Catherine was widowed and had two of her own. He took her two in, and bred her for five more. Twelve years ago, after Catherine died—neither of those Holmes girls were strong—Wally married a seventeen-year-old Mexican gal who worked on the place. Rosa. Little round gal, all tits and big shiny black eyes, and he's had nine young off her at last count. I'd say the oldest boy must be about thirty-nine by now, and the youngest maybe three or four months. Twenty of his own, and two step-kids. You take all the wives and husbands and kids and grandkids, Wally must have seventy-five kin out there, and maybe thirty or forty working around the place. And if he gives one little belch, the whole crew leaps into the air and lands looking busy. He's the he-coon out there. Pillar of the church. He's a tough, smart old boy, broad as a barn door, belly like a boulder. But he sure God ain't social. If he speaks to you, it's like it hurt his mouth. Back in the old days, when Cube and I were ripping and snorting around, Wally was behaving himself and quietly piling up the kids and the money. But like I said, if it hadn't been for Cube's estate, we'd have both sunk without a trace back there. No, boy, it couldn't have been Wally having anything to do with this."

He kept telling me that. But he kept talking about Wally. And he kept drinking. As he got drunk he spoke with more precision and walked more carefully and steadily to the bar each time.

As he let me out, he said, "You tried to kick that money into the fire?"

"I tried."

"What if it had gone right on in?"

"It would have been something to remember, I guess."

He chopped at my shoulder with a weathered fist. "It is anyway, son. It is anyway. We got you signed up. You poke around. So will I."

seven

I FOUND THE SMALL HOUSE of Juan Estobar on a quiet street in the heat of the mid-morning. It was a small frame house, freshly painted pink and white, set close to the uneven sidewalk. Under the shade of big dusty trees, some frail blades of grass struggled up through the packed dirt. There was new aluminum furniture on the screened porch. The houses were set close. There were many small children at play, birds noisy in the trees, many sounds of music, and morning television drama.

Dolores Estobar came to the screened door and looked out at me questioningly. She looked at me with frank female appraisal. She was in her middle twenties, dark and slender and very pretty. She wore navy blue bermudas and a roomy pink smock plumped with an obvious pregnancy.

"Did you want something?"

"Are you Dolores Estobar?"

"Yes, why?"

"My name is McGee. I'd like to talk to you about Mona Yeoman."

"Listen, you people have got to stop bothering me."

"It isn't like that this time."

"Then what is it like?"

"If you want to phone Mr. Yeoman, he'll ask you, as a favor to him, to talk to me for a little while, if you aren't too busy right now."

"I wouldn't know where to begin to look for her."

"You know she's gone, then?"

"Well, I guess about everybody knows that by now. About nineteen people have made a real point of telling me about it—that she took off with that Mr. Webb the day before yesterday. Mister, they don't need any newspapers in this town. I didn't know she was actually going to do that. I couldn't tell you a thing."

"There's a couple of other things I wanted to ask you about."

"Well . . . I was just ironing some. You come on in."

The furniture was bright and new, the small house extraordinarily neat. The kitchen was unexpectedly huge, and it looked like a demonstration kitchen, crammed with every electric gadget known.

"Some kitchen, huh? It was Mona's wedding present to me. She worked it out with Johnny, my husband. A surprise. When we got back from the trip, here it was. They had to move the wall there way back to make room. Look at the crazy refrigerator. It's hotel-size. You'd like a cold beer?"

"Thanks."

She gave me the beer. I sat with it at a cheery little breakfast bar. She stood in the middle of the kitchen, facing me, ironing white shirts.

"I don't know what I can tell you."

"Well, you can tell me if you were surprised when you heard it. And why you were surprised."

"I'll say I was surprised. I knew she was getting involved with that guy. But what I think she wanted, she wanted her husband to take her seriously. You know what I mean?"

"Not exactly."

"Well, Mr. Yeoman treated her like a kid. And she is a kid in a lot of ways. But him being so much older and all, when she wanted to be real serious, he was kind of laughing. Oh, he likes her a lot. Don't get me wrong about that. You know, a lot of the time even though I'm six years younger than she is, I felt older." She frowned down at the cuffs she was working on. "She gets these ideas about herself. Like she was living in a soap opera. Life isn't like that. It's too bad she can't have kids. Except for not having babies, it's a pretty good relationship. They have fun together. And old as he is, I can tell you he's plenty of husband for a girl. But I didn't think she'd actually take off. Boy, that's pretty stupid! I thought it was pretty stupid her actually going to bed with that professor. I think if I'd still been working for her, I would have talked her out of that. But I left to get married last April, and after we got back from the honeymoon she was over here practically the next day, crying and carrying on and saying John Webb was the great love of her life and he treated her like a real woman and so on. She said she could never never let Jass know she'd been unfaithful, but I knew darn well the next brawl they had she'd throw it up to him and she did. And the next time she came to see me, she still couldn't sit down without whining. I'm surprised because I know darn well she didn't get Jass to finance this trip, and she at least knows herself well enough to know she can't get along without money and lots of it, and Jass cut her off months ago. I guess they must have quarreled or something and she did it to hurt Jass. But I'll bet you by now she's scared and worried."

"I understand you and Mona had a good friendly relationship."

"Oh sure. She knew I wouldn't take advantage. Like being too friendly when anybody was around. But we didn't have any secrets. We couldn't really be friends, because I was working for her. You understand. But we talked a lot, and trusted each other. She'll be back. You tell Mr. Yeoman he can count on that. I guess he knows it already. She'll be back, and he'll make her sweat some, but he'll take her back. He'll give her one grade A thrashing, which she deserves, and take her back like before. I just don't know what's been making her act so silly. Why should she leave a man she gets along with so good? I swear, because I've seen it happen, all he ever has to do is lay a hand on her and her knees sag and she starts breathing hard."

"Maybe she didn't run off with John Webb."

"Oh, everybody knows she did."

"Dolores, there are some people who believe they didn't run off at all. There's some reason to believe they were both murdered and the bodies hidden."

The iron came to rest. She stared at me. Suddenly she snatched the iron up and took a worried look at the shirt. She set the iron on the stand and came over to the little bar. There were stools on both sides. She sat opposite me and stared at me.

"Mr. Yeoman would never never do anything like that!"

"I don't believe he would."

She bit her lip. "But who would? It doesn't make any sense!" She tried to smile. "John Webb's weird little sister . . . Mona told me all about her . . . she wouldn't have the nerve for anything like that." She shook her head. "You must be mistaken, Mister McGee, really. Everybody says they went to El Paso together."

"That was two people who vaguely resembled them."

She studied me. She was a most attractive woman—golden flesh tones, strong features, splendid dark eyes. "There'd be

no point in your telling me a lot of crazy lies, I guess. Bu
I just can't imagine Mona . . . dead. She's so alive!"

"Dolores, I'm sorry I've upset you. I thought you migh
be able to think of something useful."

"She's been stopping by to see me and tell me her trou
bles. Those tax guys worried her. That's what they were, yo
know. I'm sure they were just what they said they were
But she thought they were maybe working for Jass. Sh
wanted things to be real dramatic, always. Poor Jass. If i
turns out to be true, he'll be all broken up over it."

"Why would somebody want to make it look as if Mon
had run away?"

She looked blank. "Gee, I don't know. So they'd have a
better chance of getting away with it, I guess."

She walked out onto her front porch with me. She had a
good smile. I said, "Have yourself a prize baby, Dolores."

Her eyes turned surprisingly cool. "Only the Anglos ar
supposed to wait so long, eh? It better be twins, to catch up
We're supposed to breed at fifteen."

"Hey, take it easy."

"Maybe I don't like being patted on the head."

"Mrs. Estobar, I did not mean to offend you in any way."

"Believe me, I am through bending the humble neck, the
years I worked for the Yeomans. I say what I damn please
to anybody."

She glowered at me. Fire and iron, blood and pride. Som
Indio blood there. I couldn't help it. I laughed. In a few
moments the corners of her mouth twitched and she laughe
too. But I was glad there was no knife in her hand before
she decided to laugh.

"I'll try again. Have a happy baby. Okay?"

"Okay. He'll be happy. I promise."

But even with good temper restored, she seemed a little
bit distracted. She glanced beyond me. She seemed glad to
have me leave.

As I walked to the car I saw a heavy-duty pickup truck
parked on the other side of the street, about three door
down. It was a dusty pickup, and the two young men who
stood behind it—lounging against the tailgate, wearing work
clothes—looked big and brown and fit, their Indio-Latino
faces broad, watchful, impassive.

As I drove past them I could understand why Mrs.
Estobar wanted me to leave. On this street, at this time of
day, a strange gringo calling on the pretty housewife was an

object of suspicion. Salesman, bill collector, cop or boyfriend? Watch and wait and find out for sure.

There are too many men who feed on the minority groups, and too many ways to take advantage. So they have little ways of taking care of their own. As I turned off her street, I had the feeling that I would not have wanted those two by the truck to misunderstand my little mission.

I looked before I drove away, and she waved from the porch. I drove a half dozen blocks and phoned Yeoman's home from a drugstore. A man told me I might reach him at the office. He gave me the number. There a woman with a nasal drawling voice told me he had been in early and had left a little while ago. She asked my name and when I told her she said that I might be able to reach him at the Cottonwood Club, the Kendrick Building, the three-hundred block on East Central Avenue, use the private elevator.

It was a new office building. I had noticed it before. Glass and aluminum on stilts with pierced concrete to kill the desert glare. In the lobby was a bigger than life-size statue of a prospector leading a loaded burro, done in silver. The club elevator, labeled in very small silver script, took me to the fourteenth floor. I walked out of it into a sturdy cage of heavy steel mesh. The attendant left me in the cage while he murmured into a phone. He then pressed a buzzer which opened a door in the cage. A small man led me back through paneled baronial silences to a small elevator and took me to the sixteenth floor. He took me past shower rooms, exercise rooms, game courts, to a small gym and pointed across to where Jass Yeoman in sweat pants, stripped to the waist, was working the weights, breathing hard, sweat rolling down his chest, the tough muscles of his shoulders rolling under the brown hairy hide.

He quit when I walked up, took a towel from a hook and mopped his face. "Sweating the best bourbon, son," he said. "Waiting for the call from Charlie. How about this layout? We had a fine old club, but it set on land too valuable for it. So we sold it, tore out all the paneling and fixtures, leased these top three floors from one of Boone Kendrick's companies, and we never had it so good. Best food in a hundred miles. Two hundred. Biggest drinks, too. What have you got on your mind?"

"That it could be a game of doubles, Jass. First Mona and then you. For all the marbles you've got. Gimmicking it up made it less evident. Say she'd died in an everyday ca crash. You'd start thinking about a new will."

He swabbed his chest, slowly and thoughtfully. "Even you're dead wrong, you just earned your scorched money Trav."

"Who gets it?"

"In the event of a common disaster, it's set up to go int a little foundation, provided there's any left after they ge through picking little pieces off it. But this isn't any commo disaster. She's predeceased me. We put in a lot of miles to gether in that little airplane of mine. I don't know if th situation is covered, even. She had absolutely no blood kin The nearest I got is an old maid first cousin in Yuma. I they say it was intestate, if somebody did knock me o about now, I guess her claim would be honored, if she' dirty her paws reaching for my money. Then there's abou nine kinds of business insurance. I'd have to check that ou Tell you what. It's getting on toward lunch, you go up t the roof to the bar there and tell Armando to make you bourbon sour the way he makes them for me, and I'll b along soon."

With a little help I found my way to the roof. The chair were deep, the drink excellent, the view spectacular. I sippe the drink and wondered if I should have called on th Sheriff and done enough hinting to widen his area of specula tion. I had stayed busy. I had moved out of the Latig Motel and into The Sage. I'd gone to the bank and droppe forty-five hundred into a lock box, paying a $7.70 fee for year's rental. I like lock boxes. Before you can get to th money, you have a better chance to change your mind. had placed a call to Isobel Webb. She had said in a listles voice that she had slept too hard. She said she felt tirede than when she went to bed. It was a strange and aimles conversation, with long pauses where neither of us said word. I said I would run down and see her if I got chance, and she said, with no enthusiasm at all, that tha would be fine.

I wondered how Buckelberry was doing with the searc for the car, the search for a tall skinny man with a scarre neck, the Indian search among the rugged rocks of th nextdoor mountain to the cabin where she had died. I ha found absolutely nothing in the morning paper.

Prosperous-looking and healthy-looking men were begin ning to drift in for the pre-lunch drink, alone and in smal groups. I asked the waiter where the nearest phone was. He brought one over and plugged it in and brought me a book. I hesitated and then tried Buckelberry.

They caught him as he was leaving for lunch.

"Congratulations, McGee."

"What do you mean?"

"I had a little chat with Jass this morning. I was going to look you up and ask you not to push it too hard."

"Push?"

"For chrissake, man! That hands-off label is only good under certain conditions, Jass or no Jass. In the city limits you've got Chief Kittering to contend with. Out in the county, you've got me. If either of us find you making motions like a private investigator, we'll jam you up pretty good for operating without a state license and without county approval. One more little thing like that stewardess trick and . . ."

"Stop beating your chest, Sheriff. You're the law. I recognize that. I wondered how you were doing. And I was going to make a suggestion."

"I suppose I should be overwhelmed."

"I thought you might give Jass a little quiet protection."

"Jass? Why?"

"It's just a hunch."

"I have all the problems I need."

"Had any luck with anything?"

"Why should I tell you what . . . Well, hell, we located her car about an hour ago. Tompkins is out there now. It was about six miles from the cabin, off in the opposite direction from Cotton Corners. Off a little road under some trees. Tell Jass if you plan to see him. After it's checked out, I'll have it left at his place. There's nothing else new, but you can't tell when things will break."

"How long *can* you sit on this, Sheriff?"

"Until in my considered judgment I have enough proof to show that murder has been done, smart guy."

"If you want to leave a message for me or anything, I've moved to The Sage."

"Why not? Now that you can afford it." He banged the phone down. As the waiter carried it away, I saw Jass approaching, his strides swift and his face intent. His dark hair was spikey from his shower. He signaled Armando and dropped into the chair beside me.

"Took me longer than I thought. Charlie finally did what I pay him for."

"And?"

"One of the special groups of agents down there has been working on it for nearly a year. They're scheduled to hit me with it next February. Charlie got hold of a list of names. Statements they've taken checked off, and the ones they intended to take, left blank. Wally Rupert was checked off. Mona was on there. No check mark. A lot of other names, from way back. Stinking little clerks, son. Little people with no reason to like ol' Jass Yeoman. People ready to smear. Charlie says the minute they hit me, they'll slap paper on everything I've got to keep me from moving it out of the country. Bank accounts, securities, boxes, everything. He says they are working independent of the boys who usually work on my account down there, but with access to all back records on taxes." His drink came. He sipped it and leaned back and smiled and shook his head. "I tell you, boy, I try to stay steamed up, but I can't quite make it. Know what I dreamed last night? I was up there on the mesa road trying to find the place I buried that rabbit. I'd buried something with him that I had to have. Something important. Couldn't remember just what it was. Suppose it was my sense of self-preservation?"

"I don't know."

"God damn, how I miss that fool woman!"

"They found her car this morning, in that same area, tucked away on a back road. They'll leave it at your house after they check it out. Nothing else is new."

"I told Buckelberry we were trying to work this out together."

"I know."

"He wasn't real pleased."

"I know that too. Jass, one thing bothers me. Everybody in this town seems to know everything that goes on. But nothing's in the papers."

He shrugged. "Shouldn't bother you. Jaimie DeVrees has the paper and the TV and radio. Full of bright young kids. The first thing they learn is to go get just what they are sent to get, no more and no less. Jaimie likes a lot of initiative in handling the news they get, but he sure as hell squats on anybody that goes out and tries to find some. The way he figures it, it's a waste of money. Why try to dig up things that will be handed to you when people are ready?"

"But if Buckelberry's people find either body . . ."

His face twisted with sudden pain. "Then he'll phone Jaimie and Jaimie's people will purely cover the hell out of it. I want my girl found. I want her buried right. And whatever son of a bitch did this to me . . ." He shivered and unclamped his hands and said, "Let's go down and get us some slabs of good rare roast beef, son."

He was silent during most of lunch, and over good coffee he said, "I've got some detail work. How about along evening you and me go calling on Wally Rupert?"

"Is that the way to do it?"

"That's my way to do it. I got something to go on. What Charlie found out. I'll just push on that. I'll push hard and watch him and see if I can see anything else."

"What time?"

"You come to the house about eight, say." He stood up and dropped his napkin on the table. "I left word out front. You use this place like a charter member long as you're here."

"Thank you."

"Try to burn my money, boy, and you get to go first class."

eight

I HAD SIX FREE HOURS before meeting with Jass again. As I walked out of the Kendrick Building into the brightness of the afternoon, I had that small prickling sensation of being watched.

I moved around in appropriate ways, in and out of a drugstore, around a corner and back, and I could not pick anyone up. Everyone seemed to have that introspective innocence of total strangers. Sometimes the alarm bells go off by mistake. I could not understand why I felt vaguely disappointed to learn it was a false alarm.

Then I knew I wanted something to happen. I wanted a new factor added. The whole situation, as it stood, made very limited sense. I belonged in an arroyo, drying out behind the rocks. Jass's people should be hunting for Mona and John Webb in Mexico.

Why was it important for Jass Yeoman to believe his Mona was alive? Why was it necessary to kill her? Why had I been permitted to stay alive, and mess up all the careful planning? I had no assurance that Jass would level with me. The story would break, and soon. It would break when either body was found. And Buckelberry was doing some very earnest searching. For guns and scarred necks, for big blondes—dead and alive.

I do not believe in coincidence. I believe that if you keep moving, you expose yourself to a better chance of accidents happening, some good and some bad. And you have to have an eye for a cronkie. That is a cop word. It means someone who has been in trouble, is presently in trouble, or is about to be in trouble—either as victim or aggressor. A wise cop can pick them out of heavy pedestrian traffic flow, because they don't quite fit.

Driving back to The Sage, I had to pass the big bus station. I got caught on that corner by a light. I saw the big blonde woman come squinting out into the sun, hesitate, then turn and start doggedly trudging away, her clothes badly rumpled, hair unkempt, her stride uncertain.

Seconds later the clothing registered on me. Pale blue seersucker suit, red sandals with high heels, red purse. She was heading the wrong way for me, and I was in a center lane, so when the light changed I fought my way across the traffic and went around the block. She had made better time than I expected, and so I had to go around another block. I parked short of the corner, got out quickly and went to where I could see her coming toward me, teetering and wobbling along.

She wasn't aware of me until I stepped out in front of her. Her face looked gray and sweaty. The flesh around her eyes was smudged and puffy. Her hair showed a quarter inch of black root. She looked at me without surprise or indignation or automatic flirtation. She just stared and waited for the gambit.

"You could use a lift?"

"No, I just walk two three miles in the hot sun like this in high heels to keep in shape."

"Come in on the bus?"

"Yes. I slept hard and some spook clipped every nickel out this here purse, so I could sure use a lift, believe me. They didn't even leave me a dime to call a friend."

"My car's right around the corner."

When we reached the car and I opened the door for her, she paused and said, "You aren't trying to be real cute about anything, are you, friend?"

"I'll take you where you want to go."

She studied me for a moment, nodded to herself, and got into the car. I went around and got behind the wheel. She gave me directions. In the enclosure of the car she smelled sour and sweaty. The front of her suit was spotted. Her knuckles were soiled.

The directions took me out near my former local address. She was on one of the lateral streets, three blocks off the main highway, in an institutional-looking apartment building that seemed to be half a block long, two stories high and one room deep. She guided me around to the parking area in the rear. Rear stairs led up to a communal deck which extended the length of the building.

She got out of the car and looked at me and sucked her mouth into a bruised rosette and tilted her head. We were on a first name basis. No last names had been exchanged.

"Trav, I won't futz around with you with any games, huh? I'm next door to dead. I'm no good to anybody, right? I got to soak in a hot tub and get some sleep and set the alarm so as I can get to work by nine. They didn't like giving me two nights off, and I show up too beat, it wouldn't be so good, you know? But I bounce back pretty good. I was thinking, you come around at six tomorrow, I'll have a drink waiting, then we could eat someplace, you drop me off at work. Honest, you'll hardly know me I'll look so much better."

"I thought there might be a cold beer up there right now."

She gave a long sigh, and shrugged and said, "Come on then. But I warn you, I'm awful tired."

It was a very small studio apartment, with an unmade day-bed, characterless rental furniture. She opened me a cold beer. She poured herself a straight gin, put one ice cube in it and waited a few moments and then tossed it down, gagged, made a frightful face. Hot water roared into the small tub built into the bathroom corner at an angle. She trudged around, shedding shoes, suit jacket, pale blouse. She asked me, right on cue, if—on account of her money being taken from her purse—I could loan her a little to tide her over until payday. I said I could. She bit her lip and said, hesitantly, "Thirty, maybe?"

"Thirty is fine," I said. She took the bills and snapped them into her purse. She took another gin into the bathroom with her. She left the door ajar. When my beer was gone I got a fresh one in the kitchen alcove and pushed the bathroom door open and leaned a shoulder against the frame and drank the beer from the bottle.

She was on her knees in the little tub, sitting back on her heels, the water level coming to the white tops of her flexed thighs. With her eyes squinched shut, she was kneading her sudsy head.

I said, "Betty, you know, I was trying to remember something."

"Hah?"

"I was trying to remember where I'd seen you before."

"Well, I've been in this town three years, ever since I came out from Cleveland. And I've been working night trick at the drive-in for almost a year now, honey."

"I meant just the other day. Tell me if I'm wrong, Betty. Did you take a flight out of Carson on Monday or Tuesday?"

She rocked forward onto hands and knees, dunked her

soapy head and rinsed it vigorously. Her big pale body looked coarse-structured, muscular, durable, reasonably attractive. She sat back again, groped for a towel, shoved her wet hair back, mopped her eyes dry. Then she uncurled her legs and settled into the murky water in a sitting position.

"It was Tuesday," she said. "I dint notice you, honey."

"Weren't you with a tall skinny fellow? Dark?"

"That's right. His name is Ron. What we did, we flew down to El Paso. Let me tell you, it was a real swing. We got sort of stoned on the airplane. He knows all the cats down there. But it got too weird, you know? They start popping, they don't care what they do. That's too rich for me. I mean you have to draw a line, right? A person has to have some kind of privacy sometimes, right?"

I agreed. She yawned against her fist like a sleepy lioness. "Honest, I haven't had any sleep since Tuesday morning, not counting on the bus when I was robbed. That damned driver wouldn't do anything about it."

"Do you fly down there often?" I asked her.

"No. This was some kind of strange deal. I'd never seen that Ron before. What it was, it was a favor for a guy, and what Ron had to do, he had to find a tall blonde to fly down there with him on that flight out of Carson. Using kook names on the ticket. It was some kind of cover up, I guess. Ron met the guy in a bar. What the hell, it was a free vacation with expenses."

"Ron come back too?"

"No. From there he was going out to the Coast he said. He gave me some of the money he got. Fifty dollars. And I didn't dip into it at all, and then it got clipped on the bus. I should have spent it to save it. You just never know. Live and learn."

I decided it wasn't going to do any good to pry further. Buckelberry could do it with considerably more efficiency and speed.

She said, "Trav, sweetie, whynt you just go get comfortable and I'll be along, okay? You don't mind my hair being soppy?"

I looked at my watch. "Suppose I stop by tomorrow?"

She yawned again and nodded. "Any way you want to look at it, honey, that's best, believe me. I'm so tired I could cry."

I let myself out. I checked the number. Apartment 11. 1010 Fairlea Road. I found the mailboxes below. Elizabeth Kent Alverson, beautifully engraved on a creamy card.

I went back to The Sage and phoned Buckelberry from my

room. Fred wasn't in. I said it was important. They said they would try to get through to him. In ten minutes he phoned me. I gave him the woman's name and address and told him she was there, and that she had been the one who'd impersonated Mona Yeoman.

"For God's sake, McGee, will you *kindly* keep your nose out of . . ."

"You'd rather do it yourself, Fred. Sure."

In the ensuing silence I could sense the effort he was making to control himself. At last he said, in a gravelly voice, "I appreciate having this information."

"You are quite welcome. But I don't think you'll be able to make too much of it."

"I'll decide that."

"Certainly, Sheriff. Are there any *other* breaks in the case?"

"No!"

"Have you taken any steps to protect Jass?"

He hung up, very forcefully.

I felt displeased with myself. A smart-ass approach to a better-than-average officer of the law. With some people you start off on the wrong foot and you can't get back on balance. There was a tomcat tension between us, and I had the feeling that if we could each give and take one good smack in the mouth, we might get along fine from then on. Cop-taunting is a stupid and dangerous habit.

I stripped and showered and thought about Elizabeth Kent Alverson. A crude friendly piece. One of the great legion of the semi-pro. She wanted to ball around, and she kept telling herself you had to draw the line, dint you? But each year she'd draw it a little further.

At least I had learned that the Mona Yeoman killing wasn't as much of a gang effort as it had seemed. Betty and her Ron were apparently relative innocents. A small investment in a smoke screen. The risk had been, of course, that Ron would pocket the cash and not do the favor. The estimated number of participants was now more manageable. Maybe two could have done it.

It had to be for money. The whole area smelled of money. You could see them joshing each other about it in The Sage lobby. You could see it in the eyes of the girl at the lobby newsstand.

So find the money advantage, and it would lead you to the rifleman—or to whoever hired him. There was frantic money in this town. Maybe they expected the fossil water to run out soon. Grab it quick, and be ready to move along.

I put fresh shorts on and stretched out on the bed just as the phone rang. It was Isobel Webb.

"Travis?"

"How is it going, Isobel?"

Deep sigh. "I don't know. It's this waiting. Not knowing what to think. I don't know what to do with myself. That's why I drove up here."

"You're in town?"

"I'm in the lobby. I borrowed a car. I thought that when . . . when they find him, it will be somewhere around Esmerelda. Can you come down and talk to me?"

"Five minutes. Wait for me in the cocktail lounge."

"I'll sit in the lobby here and wait."

She stood up like an obedient child when I walked toward her. She had on a mouse gray blouse, a drab skirt, sensible shoes. She hid behind her big dark glasses. Her smile was nervous and tentative. I took her into a gloomy corner of the cocktail lounge, and she thought she would have a sherry.

"The house is so terribly empty," she said. "I keep walking back and forth near the telephone. Faculty wives are trying to be nice, but I can't stand the way they coo at me."

"They found Mona's car."

"I know. Do you mind my coming here?"

"Not at all. But I have to leave here at quarter to eight."

"Where are you going?"

"To go visit somebody with Jass Yeoman."

"I guess you don't want to tell me about it."

"It's quite complicated."

She took the glasses off and sipped her sherry. "Are you working for Jass now?"

"In a way."

"To help them all hush up whatever happened to her and John?"

"No. To find out who did it."

"What if Jass Yeoman did it, Travis?"

"Then he is the best liar I have ever met in my life."

"What . . . what if we never find out anything?" Her voice broke a little. "I don't think I could stand that. Not ever knowing. I don't know what would become of me. Don't look so worried. I'm not going to lose control. Not like yesterday. I dreamed I saw John dead. I woke up and it was still vivid. And he is dead, of course. That's why I could leave our place. I know he's never coming back there."

"Easy, Isobel."

"I'm all right. I just want to *know*."

"We'll find out."

"Oh sure. You and Mr. Yeoman and that Sheriff. You'll find out, won't you? If you don't know already."

"You get these little paranoiac impulses, Isobel. The world is not against you. There are no conspiracies against you."

"I went through John's papers today. He had a twenty thousand dollar insurance policy, a group thing through the school. I'm the beneficiary. When they find his body I'll get the money and give you half to find who did it."

"That isn't necessary."

"Do you know what I'm going to do with that money?"

"No."

"I still have that non-transferable lease. I am going back to the islands. My father changed the name of it to Webb Cay. I can get the house fixed up. I could live there on the income from twenty thousand. Forever. My God, I am sick of people. I've had enough to last me the rest of my life. I could be contented there. In this incarnation, I just didn't make it. I'll mark time and wait for the next one, Travis."

I took the drugstore tube out of my jacket pocket and put it in front of her. "Little present. It's that sun-proofing stuff for your lips."

She picked it up, peered at the label in the dim light, and then began to cry.

nine

SHE SAID she was not the least bit hungry. I took her to the grill and she ate a gigantic steak, and said it must have been the sherry. Once fed she began to yawn and her head began to sag. At quarter to eight I gave her my room key and sent her up to sack out while I went off with Jass.

I was a few minutes late. He was pacing around in his driveway. He grunted a surly welcome, and then tried to make a sports car out of his big Chrysler. We burst out of the city, hurtling north toward the bailiwick of the Rupert clan, through a cool blue night, with a faint red still visible along the western horizon.

I had one of those strange moments of unreality, that old what-am-I-doing-here feeling. I did not know this rugged old bastard, had not known his wife, had not planned this much involvement with his life. Somehow, without meaning to, I had forfeited a part of my necessary independence. I was uncomfortable in a crypto-employee role. A very strange gal was sleeping in my rental bed. And somewhere out in the blue night, a big blonde and a professor were sleeping a good deal more soundly.

"Doesn't know I'm coming," Jass mumbled.

"Oh?"

"He never goes out. He's always there in the evening."

"What am I supposed to do, Jass?"

"Stand by. Watch him. Listen to him. Later you tell me how much you believe and how much you don't."

"You know him better than I do."

"With Walter Rupert, that ain't much help."

It was twelve miles out of town, with a big ranch gate that I had to get out and open and close after Jass took the car through. We went about a half mile and came onto a great sprawled complex of ranch houses, barns, bunk rooms, outbuildings. Jass parked by the largest house and we got out. There was a night-flavor of life and movement. Lights and bits of music, the sounds of children at play, people going to and fro between other houses. Two cars left, going out the way we had come in.

A man came sauntering out of the shadows and put a light on us. "Mr. Yeoman, isn't it?"

"Want to see Wally."

"You just wait right there a minute, sir."

It was a good five minutes before he came back. "Mr. Rupert he says take you in the main house and have you wait on him. He finishes up what he's doing, he'll be along."

We followed the man into the main house, into a long room with two stone fireplaces, trophies on the wall, deep leather chairs. The man gestured toward a small bar in the corner of the room, said, "He'p yourself, gentlemen," and left us alone.

I fixed a drink for Jass and one for myself. As he took it he said slowly, "The thing is never knowing just how far he would go, one way or another. If we'd stayed locked close in a business way he'd have ate me up, slow and sure, on account of he takes pains with every little tiny thing. I had to pry myself loose. We still have a couple of small things together, but the contact on those is all through lawyers, and they're closing out a little at a time. But by God he should have had the decency to give a man warning. No matter what."

I asked a question. He didn't seem to hear it. I gave up. In a little while I heard the heavy sound of a door closing. A big old man paused in the doorway and looked in at us. He was big-shouldered, big-bellied, broad, bandy-legged. He was dressed like a country deacon, in lifeless black with a white shirt, dark tie. He stood with his chin lowered, looking out at us from under gray shaggy brows, the room lights gleaming on his baldness. His nose was hooked, his mouth large and narrow. Anthropoid arms were heavy and long. He had a masculine force about him, a great presence, born of his certainty of his own force. He was dynastic man. He was the bull-beast and this was his grassland. Three wives and a score of children seemed a perfectly natural result of this controlled energy.

"Hate to interrupt a man when he's out back someplace bailing up money," Jass said.

Rupert stared at me. He came slowly into the room. He made me feel as if I wanted to apologize for something.

"Meet Travis McGee," Jass said. "He works for me."

Rupert stared until he had finished his exhaustive inventory, and then went to the bar and fixed himself a tall glass of soda without ice. As he fixed it, he said, "I was trying to think of the last time you were here, Jasper." His voice was shocking. Apparently something was wrong with his throat. Each word was spaced, given equal weight and emphasis, as though a machine had been taught to talk.

"When Catherine died."

"Long time ago," Rupert said. He sat in one of the leather chairs, his face in shadow.

Jass leaned forward. "I come onto some information, Wally. The government is building a tax case against me. A big one. I find out you've been cooperating with them."

"Yes."

"Couldn't you've tipped me off?"

"Why?"

"Goddammit, it would have been the decent thing to do."

Rupert was silent for what seemed to me a long time. "Long ago, Jasper, we helped each other. Not out of love. We did some things. So we could survive. The things we did were dangerous. There is no statute of limitations about fraud. Now it is up to each of us to save ourself, not the other fellow. You wonder if I made a deal. Certainly. What was the deal? I testified under oath to all I could remember. The records are gone. You know that. I agreed not to inform you. I made a settlement with them. Larger than I'd hoped it would be. But I'm in the clear now, Jasper. They won't smash me or jail me. If they bring criminal charges against you, I will testify. That is part of the deal."

"You son of a bitch," Jass whispered.

"Why get emotional? What should I have done? Be a nice fellow and hurt my family to keep from hurting you? You are a silly man, Jasper. If you were careful, you would have known what they were planning and what they were doing, and maybe you could have protected yourself while there was still time. Maybe you could still run, if you plan it carefully, if you don't attract their attention while you're turning things into cash."

"I don't think I give a damn about all that," Jass said.

For the first time I sensed that Walter Rupert was very slightly off balance. "What?"

"Suppose you didn't tell them everything, Wally."

"I don't understand."

"You could have told them the stuff that makes me look

the worst, and saved the stuff that makes you look most like
a thief. Maybe, with more information, they'd come back
on you again."

"Please try to make sense, Jasper."

"They were going to talk to Mona."

"So?"

"Could she have fixed your wagon a little bit? She and
that lawyer of hers dug up some stuff."

"So?"

"They never got to talk to her."

"But they will. I think you should make sure she keeps
her mouth shut. Anything she can say will hurt you more
than me."

"You hear she'd run off with that schoolteacher?"

"Somebody said something, yes."

"She didn't. Somebody killed the both of them, and tried
to make it look as if they'd run off."

After a long silence Rupert said, "Now I know why you
wasted your time coming here. I don't have your flaw. I
don't get emotional about these things. The answer is no. If
a person was a great danger to me, if there was no other
way, I could have them killed. But there would be nothing
clumsy about it. If you know she didn't run off, this thing
must have gone wrong for someone. I would have to know
nothing would go wrong, or I wouldn't risk it. No, Jasper.
She was no danger to me. You see, when I decided to take
my gamble, I decided not to hide anything—even little
things that had nothing to do with you and that you never
knew about. Because, you see, I know you will fight. The
way it is, nothing you can tell them about me will surprise
them. I thought it all out. I am not a nice fellow, the way
you think of these things. Maybe you're not one either."

Jass stood up quickly. He glared down at Walter Rupert.
"You don't scare me, Wally. You scare a lot of people. All
these people of yours out here, you got them so scared
maybe they could go too far trying to please you. A little
hint or something, and they jump the gun. How about that?"

"No, Jasper."

"How can you be so sure?"

With eyes almost closed, Rupert said, "I know what every
one of them is doing at all times. I make it my business to
know. Some of my sons are very crafty. I'm sorry your girl
is dead. But it has nothing to do with me and mine. Goodnight, Jasper."

He didn't stand or speak or even turn his big head when we left the room.

I expected a chilling ride back to the city, but Jass drove very slowly. "What do you think?" he asked me.

"I don't know. I believe him, I guess. He . . . he seems to be an unusual man."

Jass snorted. "Unusual! One of those is all the world can stand."

"I guess he's made things pretty rough for you on this tax thing."

"It's going to be bothersome."

"No more than that?"

"It could sting a little. It could cost me. I got me a great big packing case full of old records. I'll drag it out long as I can, then when it gets real tight, I'll all of a sudden find those records. A lot of them are correct and a lot of them are part correct and a lot of them have got nothing to do with anything that ever happened. By the time that stuff gets all hashed out they'll start dickering toward a settlement. If I don't like it, I just could find two more crates full of old records in a warehouse someplace. I can keep ten CPA's and ten lawyers going for a long time. Maybe as long as I live. And then who gives a damn?"

"You must have been a great pair, you two. The fox and the weasel."

"Watch your mouth, son."

"How did the widows and the orphans make out when you two were operating?"

"They stood in line for it, boy. They always do. Ring the bell and the suckers come on the run. In this world, you either take or you're tooken. Figures lie and liars figure, and the only thing worth all the trouble is a good bourbon, a good bed and a busy woman. There are a hundred and fifty thousand new folks, net, in the world every day, and the sun will set on all but one or two of them before they can even get to lift their head. So set the hook deep while you got the chance."

"The Yeoman philosophy."

"It's worked so far."

He turned into his drive and I said, as he parked it, "It's worked fine, I guess, Jass. You're in such great shape right now."

As we walked toward the doorway of his house he said, "But think how good I had it, and how long I had it good."

"I liked you a little better when you were talking about burying a jackrabbit, Mr. Yeoman."

"Don't get the wrong idea," he said. "I loved that woman."

He had stopped in his indignation, turning toward me, and in the heavy shadows of the grounds, I saw the dark shape come plunging out of the tall shrubbery toward him, ten feet behind him and off to the side, and I caught the small flicker of reflected light from a narrow blade held low. I was very close to choking up. A knife will do that. It freezes the lower part of the gut. Astoundingly few people have the stomach even to try to use one. I let out the big bellow as I made my dive. It is a psychological weapon, unexpected and often unnerving. My shoulder bounced Jass back off the path. I feinted left and fell right, rolling and swinging my feet up at the shadowy figure. I stamped both heels into it solidly, bellowed again as I used the rebound to roll again, up onto tiptoe and fingertips, facing him. He was half down, making a gasping, grunting noise. But he gathered himself and ignored me and sped toward Jass, crouching low, blade out. Jass shot him twice in the face, and stepped aside like a matador. The figure landed heavily, coughed and spasmed once and was still. The knife tinkled along the path.

"God, I hate a knife!" Jass said in a husky whisper.

Lights were coming on. Excited voices were raised in question. Two men came running up across the yard. Floodlights went on, turned on by somebody inside the house. The two men were in uniform.

"Mr. Yeoman! Mr. Yeoman, you all right? My God, what was that terrible bellering?"

"I'm all right. I thought Fred told you to keep an eye on this place."

"We been watching it, I swear."

"Let's find out who we got here."

They used flashlights to supplement the floodlights. House servants had come out into the yard, staying a cautious distance from the body.

"Whoever he is, he's sure enough dead," one of the deputies said. "You shoot him, Mr. Yeoman?"

"Just because you see this here gun in my hand, and you see that knife he was coming at me with? What in the world would make you think I shot him?"

"Well, I was just . . ."

"Shut up," Jass said. I moved closer. They had rolled him

onto his back. He was young. His elaborate hairdo was in greasy disarray. The ruined face had that pachuco look. It went with the tight pants, the dirty pin-striped button-down shirt under the dark green satin-nylon jacket. I had seen him on a hundred corners in a dozen cities, staring at me with a combination of defiance and stupidity, standing with an indolent tomcat grace.

They went through his pockets. He had a hundred dollars, ten tens rolled into a tight cylinder and fastened with a rubber band. He had eighty-eight cents in change. He had a yellow plastic comb. He wore a gold wrist watch that told the time in all the capitals of the world. He wore black suede shoes with thick rubber soles. He wore no socks. He wore a good-luck ring of two pot-metal snakes intertwined.

"Maybe he was out of his head, all that yelling," a deputy said. "You know him, Carl? I don't know him. You know him, Mr. Yeo . . ."

"Nobody knows him," Jass said. "Get on your radio and get somebody to come haul this garbage out of my yard. This here is Mr. McGee. He saw it all. I'm just over the line so this is county business."

"Sir, you should come in and . . ."

"Fred knows exactly where to find me, and Mr. McGee and me are going to be available to answer questions any time. So you tell Fred his first order of business is to find out who this garbage is. Now hop to it! And you folks get back in the house where you belong. Miguel, you hustle some old piece of cloth to throw over this thing. Trav, let's get on in the house and have us a drink."

We went in. He slammed the door. The lights were on. A fire was laid. He squatted and lit it. Crouched there with the kindling flames marking his tough face, he grinned up at me in a sidelong way and said, "For anything your size, son, you move very nice. Very quick and tricky. Like to scared me to death, knocking me sidelong and making a sound like an old steamboat."

"You recover fast."

"I'm no gunman. You gave me three or four seconds to get ready. I've been carrying it the last few days, in this little belly holster that slips down inside my belt."

He stood up, took the gun out, checked the safety and handed it to me. I pulled my hand back. "Let's not confuse the lab boys, Jass."

He put it away. He shook his head. "That yelling."

"The idea is to make such a hell of a noise people can't think. They go on instinct then. Sometimes the instinct is to run."

"You like to kicked him to death."

"That was the general idea."

He wandered over and fixed the drinks, handed me mine. "You see if he was real serious about me?"

"He was bringing it up from the ground, and I think he wanted to put it right in the small of your back."

"You got yourself a bonus coming."

"Suit yourself."

There was a rhythmic pulse of red light in the room. He went to the window, pulled a drapery aside. "They're loading him. They don't use sirens in this kind of neighborhood."

He looked at his watch and went over to a radio on a table near the bar and turned it on, saying, "Ten o'clock news. They give the local stuff first."

The announcer said, ". . . and has been tentatively identified as Professor John Webb of State Western University at Livingston, missing since last Monday afternoon according to Sheriff Fred Buckelberry. The body was discovered earlier this evening when a county highway crew was removing a rock slide from a private road southeast of the city. The private road leads to a cabin owned by Mr. and Mrs. Jasper Yeoman. The clearing work was being done at the special request of the county sheriff, so a lab truck could be taken up to the cabin. Mona Yeoman, the attractive blonde wife of Jasper Yeoman of this city has been missing since Tuesday noon. She was last seen at the Yeoman cabin. Foul play is feared. In a brief statement, Sheriff Buckelberry said that the twin disappearances of Professor Webb and Mrs. Yeoman had been kept quiet so that his department could work on several leads in this case. Further developments are expected momentarily. The cause of death in the case of Professor Webb has not yet been determined. And now on the national scene . . . Excuse me, we have a bulletin here. Just a few minutes ago a prowler was shot and killed in the yard of the Yeoman residence. We have no other information at this time."

Jass grunted and turned the set off. "No more privacy, boy. Now we live in a store window on main street. Found him under that rock. So it was blown down, it was blown down on him. A hell of a thorough cause of death. Funny place to hide a body."

You have to assume some kind of logic in these things,

I guess. They didn't knock rocks down on him for kicks. With such a deserted cabin situation, one could assume the road wouldn't be cleared immediately. But it would be, sooner or later. And the body would be identified. See, the prof is daid! So he didn't go away with Mrs. Y. So she is daid also. And, if the lad with the knife had put it where he wanted to put it, it could all be unraveled that the wife had predeceased Jass.

ten

I FINALLY got away from the Yeoman house at twenty after eleven. Fred Buckelberry had arrived, with deputy and stenographer. He acted very tired. He had made me tell my part of it three times, He made me promise to stop by his office Friday afternoon and sign the statement. It could not have been a more obvious case of self-defense. Had Jass missed him with those two shots, he would have taken the blade in the belly.

No identification on the decedent. They were checking him out through Phoenix.

Buckelberry kept saying in a weary way, "Jass, if he was stone broke it could be one of those things. Nice neighborhood. He's looking for a car, some wallet money. But he had a hundred dollars."

And Jass kept saying in a kindly way, "Fred, I wish I could help you. But I'm just as puzzled as you are, I swear."

Just before I left, Buckelberry told me that Miss Webb had phoned him after the professor's body had been discovered. He said she'd seemed very upset and he had asked her to come in, but she had hung up on him.

So I wasted no time getting to The Sage. Though I was busy with the dangerous mechanics of fast driving in urban traffic, I could not keep my mind from random speculation about the death of John Webb, like a puppy gnawing at the edge of a carpet. When Mona Yeoman and I had clambered over that rock slide, Webb was down under there. As Jass had said, it seemed a curious place to hide a body. Obviously the road was going to be cleared. And then the body would be found. It made me wonder if it was some sort of grotesque accident. Maybe the entire murder arrangement was like one of those bloody cinema farces the British do so well. Everything goes wrong, and bodies keep falling out of the wrong closets.

If there was a plan, and if the plan was still working, then

112

the only appropriate question was to ask what the situation would be if that knife had let the life out of Jass Yeoman. Who would be ahead? Some old lady in Yuma? The Rupert clan? And was Mona's body in some other strange and obvious place?

I put the rental car in the hotel lot and stopped at the desk and picked up the other room key. There were no messages. I went up and let myself into the room. Isobel lay on the further of the two three-quarter beds. The desk lamp was on, a weak bulb in an orange shade. She slept atop the spread, dressed except for her shoes, a yellow blanket over her. I could see a note on hotel stationery on the green blotter under the desk lamp. I decided I would let her sleep, even if the note directed me to awaken her. I closed the door soundlessly, and went quietly to the desk.

It was a curious note. No salutation and no signature. "There doesn't seem to be much point in it any more. I might have more luck the next time around. After everything is settled up, please give what's left to the scholarship fund at SWU."

After the moment of horrid comprehension, I reached her in three long strides. Her hands were slack and icy. The heartbeat was very slow, respiration agonizingly slow. I shook her and slapped her and got a faint drugged whine of protest. I got to the phone and asked to have a doctor sent up just as quickly as they could manage it. I asked for a pot of black coffee. Cursing her, I turned on every light in the room and the bathroom. I picked her up and took her into the bathroom. She was limp as a rag doll. I jounced her and shouted at her. I sat her on the floor in the corner by the tub, then used my shaving bomb to hastily mix a glass of warm soapy water. I knelt by her, clamped her jaws open, tilted her head and poured it into her throat. Some of it spilled down her sweater, but I saw her throat work with a labored slowness as she swallowed. At least she had that reflex left. I was not certain she had enough. I mixed another glass and got about half that down her. I picked her up and put her, belly down, over the rim of the tub. I knelt beside her and, holding her there, reached around and stuck two fingers down her throat. I prodded at the soft base of her tongue, and as I began to despair, I suddenly felt the musculature there begin to tighten. Then soft heavy spasms began, a dulled heavy gushing of soapy water soured by the stomach contents. When she stopped, I stimulated the spasms again, more readily the second time. I wondered where the hell they kept their doctors.

I hauled her off the tub and turned her, sat her slumped against the tub and stripped her, wasting no time in saving her clothing. I popped straps and tore fabrics. Her bra, pants and half-slip were as unadorned and sensible as her walking shoes. I turned on the cold shower spray to rinse the tub out, drawing the shower curtain partway. Then I picked her up and sat her in the tub, adjusting the tilt and apertures of the shower head so that a good solid gout of cold water smashed her in the face and torso. She rocked her head from side to side and made almost inaudible mewling noises, over the roar of the shower.

When the authoritative knock came at the door, I went to answer it, shoving her note into my pocket as I passed the desk. He was a round pink man with a sad, sagging, weary face. I led him into the bathroom. She had slumped further. I turned the water off. He took a towel and wiped her face roughly. As he checked her pulse, thumbed her eyelid up, I told him exactly what I had done.

"What'd she take?"

"I don't know."

"See if you can find what it was in."

I found the plastic bottle in the wastebasket beside the desk. There was no drugstore label on it. I took it to him. There was a little white powder in the bottom of it. He shook it out into the palm of his hand, snuffed at it, moistened a fingertip, tasted the powder. "Barbiturate," he murmured. The girl made a snoring sound. He muttered to himself, dug into his open case, found a disposable hypo, a rubber-top vial of amber fluid. He pulled one of the girl's arms over the side of the tub, alcoholed a place above the elbow, filled his hypo, made a deft injection.

"Better off in a hospital," he said, getting up off his knees.

"Is it necessary?"

"She your wife?"

"No. Doctor, if she is in danger of dying, of course she should go to a hospital. Listen, this is a very neurotic kid. Her name is Webb. They found her brother's body this evening."

He raised one tired eyebrow. "I heard about that."

"I work for Jasper Yeoman. I've gotten acquainted with this girl. I think if a big hospital thing is made of it, she's going to try to live up to the billing. If it can be passed off, like a casual thing, like a small accident, I think it can work out better for her. That is, if she isn't in danger."

He leaned against the sink, frowning. As he was about to speak, the coffee came. I think it turned the trick. He nodded approvingly.

"I gave her a stimulant. Let's see if we can make her walk."

We lifted her out. I got my robe on her and belted it. It trailed on the floor behind her. The doctor gave her three brisk slaps in the face. He put his mouth next to her ear and said, "You have to walk! Come on! Walk!" I supported most of her weight. She came along, head lolling, working her spaghetti legs.

"That's good," he said. "Keep her moving. Pour coffee into her. Don't let her drowse off. Use the cold shower again if you have to. Make her talk. Count to a hundred. Alphabet. Anything. What I wonder is, can I depend on you?"

"Yes."

He studied me, lips pursed. "I'll come back here at four in the morning. Then, if she looks all right, we'll let her sleep. By then she should be begging to sleep."

"Thank you, Doctor."

"You did pretty good before I got here. I'll stop at the desk on the way out. They act uneasy down there. You're registered as a single." He permitted himself the first small smile. "I'll say the magic word. Yeoman. They'll leave you alone. Here's my number. If she starts to get away from you, so you can't get any reaction, call me at once. This is a risk for me, too. No, don't stop. Keep walking her." He started toward the door and hesitated, looked uneasily at me. "She's a very pretty girl."

"Necrophilia never appealed to me, Doctor."

The precision of the word heartened him. He bobbed his head and left. I walked the girl. I hustled her along, giving her more of her own weight to support, catching her when she started to fall. I slapped her and jounced her. I poured steaming coffee into her. I shoved her under the shower. Her whining became more audible and bitter and abused. She was a lump. A thing. An irritating and tiresome chore. She padded and lurched and grumbled in a voice so slurred I could not make out a word. Her head bobbed loosely. This was the monstrous selfishness of self-destruction. Somebody else has to pick up the pieces.

For a long time, an hour or more, I could be ironically

amused by the doctor having called her a pretty girl. She was a doughy, dull, fatty, blue-white, flaccid thing, with her water-pasted hair, sagging mouth, slitted empty eyes. I could stand her under the water and she would take it like an obedient sow, flat-footed and streaming. I got pretty good at pouring coffee into her. And I could keep her in her floundering trudge by holding one arm. Suddenly it changed. She had begun to get wobbly again, and I put her under the shower, holding her there by one hand on her shoulder. This time she tautened. Her body seemed to lift for the first time and come alive as the cold water made her arch her back and tighten her muscles. Suddenly I realized that this was a marvelous female body, sleek, rounded, strong, flawless, with hips and breasts and belly of a ripeness that enhanced the narrow litheness of her waist. I bundled her back into the damp robe a little sooner than I had planned. She shivered for a little while, and I took that as sufficient reason not to try the shower routine again.

But by three in the morning, I had the feeling that I needed to get her past one more obstacle in the road back to awareness. She acted like a drunk. Querulous, mumbling, cross, indignant. But she seemed to have no real grasp of who she was or where she was or who I was. I kept thinking that I ought to be able to think of some way of shocking her back to reality. I brought her to a halt. She stood there swaying, eyes barely open. I closed the bathroom door. There was a mirror on the back of it. I put her in front of the mirror. I unbelted the robe and slipped it off her shoulders and tossed it aside. She stood looking at herself without comprehension. We looked odd in the mirror, all the rawboned height of McGee standing next to and slightly behind the pale perfection of the naked girl, so small in her bare feet, her frank breasts revealed, and, nested into the smoothness of her thighs, the sooty-soft-dark cornerstone to the soft and tender arch of hips. Her hair was a clotted tangle, half masking one eye. Smirking at her mirror image I put my lips close to her ear and said, "See the pretty girl? See the pretty pretty girl?"

Her eyes were stubborn slits. She swayed and sighed, then quite suddenly her eyes opened wide. Her body tightened. She bent slightly from the waist, covered her parts with one hand and flattened her other arm across her breasts. Knock-kneed, she turned and backed away from me, making a little hissing sound.

"Pretty girl?" I said.

"What . . . what are you doing to me?" Her face was chalk white.

I threw the robe at her. "I'm trying to keep you alive."

She fumbled herself hastily into the robe. "But . . . but I took all of them!"

"Yes you did, dear girl."

"John is dead."

"Keep walking."

She wouldn't until I started toward her. And then she began trudging back and forth, eyeing me with grave suspicion.

"I'm very tired, Travis."

"Keep walking."

"What time is it."

"After three. Walk faster."

"Please let me lie down, just for a minute. Please."

"Keep walking."

"My God, you're cruel. I'm sick. I'm terribly sick. I have to lie down. Really!"

"Walk by yourself, or I'll walk you."

I sat on the foot of the bed. She kept well out of my reach each time she passed me. When she began to soften again, when her eyes began to blur, I reached out and gave her a brisk clout on the fanny. It energized her.

She wept for mercy. I showed none. She faked a faint, but came out of it with alacrity when I began to peel the robe off her. She cursed me. I did not know she had such an extensive vocabulary. She cursed, whined, cried, faked, begged. But she walked. Yes indeed. She kept on walking.

O she was pitiful indeed, those eyes smudged so dark, huddled small in the robe, hating me, choking the coffee down, calling me a degenerate, demanding to know why she had not been permitted to die. Life was empty. Must she be bullied, shamed, slapped, jounced, beaten, smirked at? Yes, dear. Keep walking. Just keep walking.

Doctor Kuppler returned at four fifteen. When she realized he was a doctor, she began to recount a long and tearful bill of particulars. He ignored her completely, examined her, grunting with approval. He had her sit on the edge of the bed.

"I demand my rights!" Isobel said. "Get the police!"

Doctor Kuppler smiled sweetly at her, put one pink finger against her shoulder and pushed. She toppled over backwards, sighed once, and then began to emit a small, regular, purring snore. At his suggestion, I picked her up. He opened the bed up. I dropped her in and he covered her over.

"Nice response," he said. "Attractive young lady. Maybe it all wasn't necessary, but it's nice to be on the safe side."

"What do I owe you?"

"Considering everything, I think a hundred dollars would be just about right."

I gave it to him and asked him how long she should sleep.

"As long as she can," he said. "If she sleeps well into this afternoon, fine. Are you going to stay here too?"

"I'm exhausted, Doctor, and she's already compromised."

As the windows were beginning to get that pale look, I put the chain on the door, brushed my teeth and kissed her on the forehead and went to bed. I was no longer irritated with her. I felt proud and pleased about her. Samaritan McGee, savior of doomed womanhood. I had a curious feeling of ownership. Now you belong to me, dear girl, and damn foolishness will not be countenanced in the future. You hear?

eleven

THE ROOM PHONE woke me at noon, and I got it before it disturbed Isobel. She slept with her back toward me, looking small under the yellow blanket, just the dark crown of her head showing.

It was Jass on the phone. I told him to hold it a minute. She seemed to be too motionless. I went around her bed and bent over her. She was sleeping sweetly. I went back to the phone.

"What's on your mind, Jass?"

"You just wake up?"

"I had a busy night."

"Doing what?"

"I'll tell you later."

"Well . . . the thing I called about . . . I don't know. A man gets to thinking, after somebody nearly gets him with a knife. Should anybody hate me that much? I lay wondering in the night. Making lists. The funny thing about hate, maybe the ones you think have no call to hate you so much, the ones you've done things for, maybe that's where the hate is strongest, Trav."

"You thought of somebody?"

"Cube Fox and I used to raise particular hell up and down this country. I always figured myself for a man who'd take his fun and pay the bills for it as they come along."

Quite suddenly I remembered that pair at the gas station when I had walked out after seeing Mona slain. I remembered the man saying, "There's maybe forty grownup people running around this end of the state with Cube's blue eyes and the rest of them Mex. Cube was plain death on Mex gals."

Jass said, "I wasn't rightly in Cube's league. But you take those warm nights, and some of those country dances, and the smell of cedar scrub burning, and some belts of mescal, and the big open cars we'd run around in, and all the little warm brown gals, giggling and cuddly, and Cube and me speaking the language and all . . ."

His voice trailed off. "Do you have any particular bastard child in mind?" I asked him.

"No. No. I didn't keep track. Last night I was trying to recall. There was five or six times when I got called on to help out. I suppose there were others got theyselves married off fast, soon as they had a suspicion. And others too proud to ask. They asked and I helped out. I'd set it up quiet for them, so they could get money right from the bank. Three times it was that way, instead of just a piece of money paid out and that being the end of it. Fifty a month. Forty. To help out with the kid. It was a long time ago. I guess I could track the records down. Sanchez. Fuegos. Those are the only two names come to mind. Boy babies. They should be near thirty years old now. I don't know, son. It was something I was thinking on in the nighttime. I guess there could be some hate."

"There could be."

"Then there's the one I kept track of, but I wouldn't want to say the name over the telephone, and anyway, there wouldn't be any hate there, nothing like that. What you do, boy, you come over to the Cottonwood Club, say in an hour. I've been sloppin' around the house here, thinking of old times, missing my girl bad. I'll get dressed and see you there."

As soon as I hung up, it rang again. Isobel stirred and made a little growly sound in her sleep. It was Buckelberry. He told me the Webb girl had disappeared. He wanted to know if I had any idea where she might be. I hesitated and told him she was staying at The Sage. He wanted to talk to her. I told him she was under sedation. I told him I'd have her get in touch. He accepted it, with a certain reluctance. I told him I'd be in to sign the statement about the fellow with the knife later on. He said they had an almost positive identification on him from Phoenix. Francisco Pompa, age nineteen, delinquent, pimp and addict, and they had raised his prints on a stolen car found parked a quarter mile from Jass's house.

Isobel slept on. After I was shaved and dressed, I picked her clothing up, all of it, including her sensible shoes, and bundled it in her stale sweater. I noted the shoe size imprinted inside a shoe. 5 B. I found a maid working in a nearby room. I told her not to disturb the girl in my room. I gave her the clothing, saying that once it was cleaned up and repaired, she might know somebody who would have some use for it. She was delighted.

I had a quick breakfast, then went to the desk and checked her in, officially. Cousin Isobel. The clerk was supercilious. I smiled at him. I made it a very sleepy smile. It was not long before he became a little bit jumpy and nervous. When he was sufficiently polite, I turned away. As I had time to spare, I went to the shops on the lower level. I found a freckled little clerk with a sincere desire to please. She decided a size ten would be about right. We picked out a frivolous little orlon suit, and some very ornate and sexy yellow underthings, and a sunback blouse that would go well with the suit. She ducked next door with me and picked out some tall-heeled pumps that would go with the suit. I left the packages in the room, with a note telling her I would be back by three thirty, and if she woke up before then, order up some food and phone Buckelberry. I said I hoped the stuff in the boxes would fit.

While I was engaged in such frivolities and pseudo-sex-play in the perfumed world of woman's wear, Jasper Yeoman was busily engaged in what is sometimes termed shuffling the mortal coil. He made hard work of it. From what I learned later, I was able to reconstruct it. While driving his big car from his home to the Cottonwood Club, he began to have a feeling of suffocation, a difficulty in breathing. Alarmed, he turned into the parking lot of a huge glossy shopping center, aiming toward a gleaming drugstore as the nearest possible source of help. He parked very badly, and scrambled out of the car. By then he had begun to have uncontrollable muscle twitches. Probably the housewives, trucking foodstuffs to their cars, thought they were seeing a mid-day drunk, this big spare leathery fellow lurching and hopping and skittering, mouth wide to suck air.

On the broad walk in front of the drugstore the first of the titanic convulsions took him. He bounced and jarred, jackknifed and fell, like a puppet dangled by a cross child. On the grey cement, amid the gum wrappers and filter tips, the body arched backward, the head jerked, the neck became stiff. He rested on head and heels, face congested, countenance anxious, eyes staring, lips retracted and livid, jaws clenched.

They gathered at a safe distance and stared blankly at his agony. A clerk ran out and ran back in and called an ambulance. The convulsion ended and he slackened, rested a moment, and then asked in a weak and lucid voice if someone would help him get up. They got him up and walked him into the drugstore. Several minutes later the next convulsion took him, and he ripped himself out of their grasp and smacked and bucked against the patterned plastic tile of the retail floor.

Again he was lucid, but weaker. He went into a third one as they were loading him into the ambulance. He had the rest of them at regular intervals in the hospital emergency room, the convulsions seeming to grow stronger as he became weaker. After forty minutes, despite all attentions they could give him, he died of a combination of asphyxia and exhaustion. By then the toxicologist was quite certain of what he would find. After autopsy procedures, with intestinal contents, stomach contents, brain, liver, blood, urine, hair packed in clean glass containers for laboratory analysis, it was found that he had ingested an estimated .2 grams of strychnine, double the fatal dosage, had probably swallowed the poison within thirty minutes of the first convulsion, and had taken it in something that probably masked the very bitter taste, possibly some very strong black coffee.

But I pieced this all together later. I went to the club and waited for him. Then in some mysterious way everyone there knew he had been taken sick, knew he was at the hospital. He died ten minutes before I got there.

twelve

THERE WAS a jurisdiction problem, the officials of city and county each hoping it belonged to the other one. Careers can be blasted by the mishandling of the smallest details when an important man has died. The county, and Fred Buckelberry, were stuck with it.

He intercepted me in the hospital parking lot. He looked at me with what could have been interpreted as fond approval. I knew better. With Yeoman dead I had no clout left. He looked at me the way a cat might look at a fresh fish. He attached Deputy Homer Hardy to me, with instructions to go with me to the hotel, collect the Webb girl, take us both to the county courthouse, hold us there—voluntarily of course —awaiting Buckelberry's convenience.

We were at The Sage by ten of three. Hardy had no intention of waiting in the lobby. He waited in the corridor, outside the room door. The boxes were empty. The bathroom door was closed. I could hear water running. I tapped on the door. She said just a minute.

In five minutes she came out. Everything seemed to fit. From the neck down she was first class girl, the little suit and blouse showcasing what she had a tendency to hide. The drab wings of hair concealed her forehead. She had put on her big dark glasses. Her lips were without color, her face slightly puffy. The impenetrable lenses stared at me.

"Where are my clothes?"

"How do you feel?"

"Where are my clothes?"

"I threw them away."

"And bought me this cheap, vulgar, obvious outfit. Thank you so much."

"It wasn't cheap."

"It's cheap in a way you couldn't possibly understand, Travis."

"Honey, if you don't care whether you live or die, what

123

difference does it make what you wear? Did you get anything to eat?"

"No."

"We have to go to Buckelberry's headquarters."

"I am not going there. I'm going home."

"There's a deputy in the hall to make sure we both go there."

She was looking at herself in the mirror, hitching at the skirt. She stopped and stared toward me. "Why?"

"Jass Yeoman is dead."

"What has that got to do with me?"

"Perhaps nothing. Buckelberry wants to make sure."

"I don't understand."

"Somebody's hired hand tried to get him with a knife last night. They missed. So somebody poisoned him this noon."

"Poisoned?" she said in a faint voice.

"It wasn't a very easy way to die."

She put her fingertips to her throat. "I'm sorry about that. I . . . I hated him for not having the pride and decency to keep his wife away from my brother. But . . . poison is so ugly."

We went down in the elevator with the deputy. I told him we had to eat. He thought it a very dubious idea. Isobel told him that if she couldn't eat, she was going to lie down in the lobby and he could carry her to the courthouse.

We went to the grill. He sat with us. I asked him to go get his own table. He was very gloomy and hurt about that. He took one by the door. I ordered a steak sandwich. She ordered a large orange juice, two broiled hamburgers with everything, a side order of home fried potatoes and a pot of coffee.

I watched her as she began to eat her way steadily through the order. The silence between us seemed to get more obvious by the moment. I reached quickly and took the dark glasses off. She tried to snatch them back. "Please," she said. Her eyes looked naked, shifty, shy.

"Stop hiding and you can have them back."

"Hiding? What can I say? I haven't even thought it out yet. I can't. Believe me, I try to think about it and my mind just sort of . . . veers away from it."

"Do you still want to kill yourself?"

She looked around hastily and said, "Ssh! I . . . no, I don't think so. I don't know."

"Are you glad I stopped you?"

"I guess so. Thanks. Stupid word to say—thanks. I just thought . . . take the capsules and just . . . go off to sleep and that's the end of it. But I suppose that even if you understood, if you found me in time, you couldn't let it happen. I mean I don't resent it, because you'd have to try. Anyone would."

Suddenly I did not want her understanding. A man who had wanted to live was dead. She had wanted to die, and she sat there chomping hamburg. I suppose I should not blame her for a self-involvement that, in contrast, seemed the ultimate silliness. But, all moral judgments aside, Jasper Yeoman had been one hell of a fellow. He had been a whole man, and this was just about half of a girl.

She was sensitive to the nuance, to a flavor of disapproval, and her head tilted slightly, one eyebrow arching. "Something is wrong?"

"Everything is nifty, Iz."

"I hate that nickname. I . . . I can't remember everything very clearly." I saw pink suffuse her face. "But . . . I was nude?"

"The colloquial expression is bare-ass."

Pink turned to angry red. "How can you be so crude and indifferent?"

I looked away from her, shrugged one shoulder. "Eat your starch, honey. The deputy is getting restless. About the side show, I was trying to shock you awake. It worked. Just don't assume it was such a tremendous deal for me. You've got the standard equipment in the standard places. Nothing gaudy happened. I was saving your life. All that blundering and gagging and whoopsing around didn't make me feel particularly romantic."

She sat scrunched and pallid, eyes downcast. It was a cheap little victory, as most of the easy ones are. So I gave her back her glasses, but her appetite was gone. She walked out with me as if she was trying to hold a coin in place between her knees. Homer Hardy took us to a small room off the courthouse corridor. He told us to bang on the door if we needed anything. He closed it and left us there.

There wasn't much left for us to say to each other. Time went by very slowly. There was a lot of traffic in the corridor, a lot of voices.

Out of a long silence I said, "There'll have to be arrangements about your brother."

"I've been thinking about that. Our parents were cremated. John would want that too. There's an old family plot in Weston, New Hampshire. A simple memorial service in the university chapel, I think. There's a man in Livingston —I guess I just arrange for the authorities to release the body to him, and tell him what I want. But I don't know how they get the urn from here to Weston, how that's done. I guess the man can tell me. Then, there's the insurance too."

"Can I help in any way?"

"Thank you, no."

"How do you feel?"

"Tired. And empty."

A room without windows seems to slow the passage of time. Overhead fluorescence in an eggcrate housing. Green tin chairs, raggedy old magazines, an almost sickening sweetness of some spearmint deodorant which masked all the lesser stinks of authority. She sat behind her big dark lenses, her white knees and white ankles pressed neatly together, hands folded on her purse.

It was five of six by my watch when Hardy came in and took her off to talk to Buckelberry. Half an hour later he sent for me. I was astonished to find him alone. The statements were ready. I read one over and signed the three copies necessary.

He took his time lighting a pipe, tamping it, relighting it, making um-pah sounds as he got it going to his satisfaction.

"They're all screaming for blood," he said. "Kendrick, Gay, O'Dell, DeVrees, Madero . . . all of them. Jass was one of theirs."

"And it would scramble your future, Fred, if you came up empty?"

His glance was sharp and unfriendly. "I'm not too worried about that. It all got too messy. The question is how to come up soon. Anything so complicated has to fall apart. But I want to look good, McGee. I want to look very very good."

"What are you trading?"

"I've got a very wide open vagrancy ordinance, and some understanding judges. You can swing a brush hook in the hot sun for ninety days. I like that ordinance. It makes the job easier."

"I can imagine," I said, and stood up.

"Where you going?"

"Let's go see one of those judges."

"For God's sake, sit down!"

I sat. "I can't be pushed that way, Sheriff."

He studied me. "You'd do the ninety days?" He sighed. "Yes, I guess you would."

"How did they give it to Jass?"

"In strong coffee. He liked it boiled, black and bitter. They'd make a thermos of it so it would stay hot on him while he pooted around showering and shaving and so on in the morning. The little bit left was loaded with strychnine. The cook made it and took it in to him. She's cleared. You know how that place is built. He had private dealings. Some people didn't want to be seen going there or leaving. That side door to the study. He carried the coffee down there, phoned you from there. He say anybody was with him?"

"No."

"He have any ideas about who was after him?"

I'd a long silent time in a small room to think about it. I had no reason to get mysterious with Buckelberry. But I had so little to go on, such a vague little hunch.

"Well?" Fred said.

"Jass started wondering about his children, Fred."

He stared at me. "Don't get cute. He didn't have any."

"Not officially." I told him what Jass had told me of the old days. Buckelberry listened intently. And with a cop instinct he jumped on the same idea I'd had.

"How about the one he kept track of, the one that couldn't hate him?"

"He didn't give me the name. Who would know?"

Buckelberry didn't answer me. He stared into space and then he banged his hard fist on his desk. "Suppose," he said softly, "just suppose we come on Mona dead a long time. Then we bury the two of them, Jass and Mona. And the will comes to probate and some son of a bitch steps forward with *proof*, with absolute *proof* he's Jass's illegitimate kid. Could he inherit? I don't know the law on that. What if he had letters from Jass? He'd be the closest blood relative for sure."

"And he'd be free to go see Jass at any time."

Buckelberry nodded grimly. "Like about noon today."

"Maybe he wouldn't dare come forward now," I said.

"Why not?"

"This whole plan just got too screwed up, Fred. Nothing worked the way it was supposed to. Maybe all that was left was the hate."

"It's a starting place anyways," he said, sighing.

"How about your other starting places?"

He shook his head. "Can't find that Ron. Can't find the other body. Can't get a line on the rifle. The Alverson woman was a dead end. Webb's body gave us no leads." He stretched and rubbed his face and reached for the phone. "Now let's see if any of those eager old pals of his knows anything." He paused and said, "Set outside for a while, McGee."

"I'll help out in any way I can. He paid me some money. I haven't earned it yet. I'd like a chance to."

He pulled his hand back from the phone and studied me. "Some people have a knack. Wherever you go, damn you, something seems to happen. You're going to meddle anyways, aren't you?"

"Unless you give me ninety days."

He opened a bottom drawer, fished and clanked around in it, came up with a shiny something and flipped it at my face. I got my hand up in time and the chrome badge smacked into it.

"Raise your right hand and repeat after me."

"Just like a western?"

"Exactly like a western, McGee. I'm authorized."

I swore. I was official. I put the badge in my pocket. Temporary Deputy Travis McGee. I could officially get myself killed in line of duty and receive certain death benefits as provided by Esmerelda County, and until relieved by the Sheriff of said county, I would receive pay of five dollars per month or fraction thereof. I signed the official register. And went out to wait outside.

As I went out, Isobel stood up from the corridor bench with a humble and obedient manner.

"What do you want?"

She drew me aside. "Travis, . . . I thought you might drive me back to the university, if it wouldn't be too much trouble."

"They run buses."

"Please. If you don't, it would . . . look strange. I told the Sheriff you would. I . . . didn't tell him anything about what I did." The blush came oozing up from the neck of her new blouse. "So he thinks I . . . we . . . it was . . . He thinks it . . ."

"He must have a vivid imagination, honey."

"Please don't be cruel. I . . . made the arrangements, some

of them, about John. And I just don't want . . ." She dropped the humble manner, stepped back, lifted her chin and said, "Damn you, I'd rather not be alone. If you can't understand why . . ."

"Okay, okay, okay. But I have to hang around for a while. I'll drive you down. Or you can come back to the hotel. You're registered, cousin."

"Cousin?"

"I had to tell the desk something."

She walked to the bench and sat abruptly and said, "I can never go back there as long as I love . . . *live!*"

"Your Freudian slip is showing."

"That's a stale, tiresome, shopworn remark. And you are a boor."

"Now you're acting more like yourself, honey."

She asked me if I was under detention or arrest. I showed her my new badge. She shook her head as if the world had gone mad.

We waited. I got us some cokes out of a machine. I bought a paper. Jass had made page one. Reporters discovered us and swooped in, blinking their flash units, asking simultaneous questions, and I hustled Isobel into an alcove off the communications center, where they could not follow. We were Sister of Slain Professor, and Mystery Figure.

At last Buckelberry appeared, a paper cup of coffee in his hand. He leaned against the alcove wall and looked down at us.

"You tell her what we're checking now?" he asked.

"No."

"When can he take me home?" Isobel asked.

"Miss Webb, did your brother ever say anything to you about something Mrs. Yeoman could have told him? About any illegitimate children Jass Yeoman might have?"

"Certainly not!"

"Don't get so indignant at every little thing, Miss Webb. He could have told you something like that to justify his relationship with Mrs. Yeoman."

"I wouldn't have listened to that kind of specious reasoning."

"No, I don't guess you would have, at that." He turned away, saying, "McGee, come look at the map a minute."

I followed him into his office. He put his thumb under

the name of a tiny place northeast of Livingston. It was called Burned Wells.

"As long as you're taking her back down there, you can check this one out. Listen, I've gotten more loose talk and rumor than I know what the hell to do with. Tomorrow we can start checking out bank records, hoping Jass didn't cover the back trail too careful. Fish Ellery says there's a woman down there Jass was more serious about than most. He says it was probably twenty-five years ago, before Cube died. He says she was seventeen or eighteen then, Mexican with a lot of Indio blood, a very fierce sort of proud girl. That would make her forty-two or three now. He remembers her first name was Amparo. He says Jass nearly lost his head over that one. Took her on trips with him, bought her a lot of stuff, kept her around for maybe a year. It isn't much to go on, but it's a very small place."

"It doesn't look like much of a road going in there."

"It's fifteen miles dead end off State Road 100. What it is, it's a village of people that do some ranch work on those spreads beyond there, out of my county. Hughes, Robischon, Star B. It's smaller than it was. The young ones leave. Shacks and a store. Gas pump and a 'dobe church. That Amparo could be long dead, or moved away. Or still there and not about to tell anybody anything. But it's worth taking a look."

"I hope you have better leads than this one."

"I do. I've got men working them. You come back here with whatever you can find out. I'll still be here."

thirteen

AT EIGHT THIRTY I stopped with Isobel at a motel restaurant at the south edge of town. I told her of the new direction of the investigation, what Jass had said, and what the Sheriff had given me to do. Her response, if any, was very muted.

"Aren't you interested?" I asked her.

"I guess so. Travis, I'm emotionally exhausted. It's been such a strange day. All that waiting. Like in an airport when everything is grounded. Yes, I want to know who killed my brother. It seems to me now he died years ago. Or even that I knew he was going to die. He was the innocent bystander, I guess." She frowned across the table at me, dark glasses laid aside. "There is something strange about trying to kill yourself. You do kill some part of yourself, no matter what. Maybe the ability to feel deeply. I don't know. I feel like a stranger to myself. I have to find out who I am, who I am going to be. I feel . . . cut loose from everything. And I have this strange little feeling of . . . some kind of unholy joy. Every once in a while. An electric sparkle, like knowing you're soon to go on holiday. I shouldn't feel like that for no reason. I keep wondering if something is . . . wrong with my mind."

"I'll make an absurd guess. Maybe you're glad to be alive."

"Not particularly. But I won't try to kill myself again."

On my road map the fifteen miles over to Burned Wells was a faint dotted blue line, heading east off State Road 100 about six or seven miles north of Livingston. I slowed so I could spot the turn, pick up some landmark so I could find it easily on my way back.

"Let me go over there with you," she said.

"Why?"

"I don't know. It's something to do. If you find her, maybe she'd talk to me more readily than to you."

I took her along. It was a narrow sand and gravel road through burned land under a starry sky so bright I could

131

see the contours of the land on either side of us. We climbed into a coarse jungle of huge tilts of rock, small buttes rising out of sand and cactus, and the road found its windy way through this Martian pasture. The car thumped and slewed and churned along, with my headlights picking up the infrequent wink of a beer can, the red eyes of a jackrabbit. The road moved down again to a broad valley floor, past solemn stands of pipe organ cactus, and straightened toward a faraway glimmer of small lights against a black hill flank on the far side of the valley.

The village of Burned Wells was one broad unpaved street two blocks long. It had gone to bed for the night. The lights we had seen came from the white hissing glare of gasoline lanterns. One hung from the porch roof of the store, where a small group of men sat on the steps and railing and porch chairs. They were drinking beer. There was a portable radio on the porch railing, turned to a volume the speaker couldn't handle, so that the highs buzzed and the bass blared, playing country music. I stopped short of the gas pump and got out of the car. When I was halfway to the porch the music stopped abruptly. There were nine of them, all middle-aged or older. The lantern made brilliant highlights and impenetrable shadows, leaching out all color so that the group, silent and motionless, looked like a black and white print which had been developed for maximum contrast.

I stopped short of the porch and said, "Good evening."

No response. Unless somebody spitting over the railing is a response.

"Perhaps you can help me."

No response.

"I am trying to find a woman who lived here twenty-five years ago. I do not know her last name. Her first name was Amparo. She used to know Jasper Yeoman."

Two of them spat. Maybe I was achieving better communication. They were a hardy-looking group, rough work clothes, tough weathered faces, bodies thickened by hard labor.

"Jasper Yeoman was killed today."

That created a stir, a moving, a few secretive mutterings.

"I worked for him," I said. "On private matters. I think it would be better if I didn't have to come back here with the county sheriff to help me get information about her."

A man bent down into the shadows beside his chair. He

muttered something. A small boy I had not seen sprang up, went lithely over the railing and went running down the road into the darkness, bare feet slapping the packed dirt.

"Is she still here?" I asked.

"You wait," the oldest one said.

It was not a long wait. The boy was back in about three minutes. He went right to the old man and whispered to him. It seemed a very long message.

"You can see the woman," the old man said. "Her man gives his permission. The child will take you."

I got Isobel out of the car, and we followed the boy down the middle of the wide dark street. When my eyes were used to the darkness I could see the small church at the end of the main street. Dogs came running out to bark at the scent of strangers. We turned left at the church. The boy pointed at an adobe house and ran off without a word. The door was open. There was a flicker of orange light inside. The small front garden was guarded by twisted sticks painted white. I rapped on the open door.

A woman appeared and stared at us and backed away and said, "Come in." Her voice was harsh. It was an order. The room was small and bare. Doorways led to other rooms.

"I am Mrs. Sosegado," she said. "I was with Jass Yeoman a long long time ago. You sit down, please."

She was a short woman. She looked almost as broad as she was tall, but muscular rather than fat. Her hair was shining black, her face the color of a penny, her features so harsh and strong she looked masculine. Big breasts and hard belly pushed against the flowered fabric of a faded cotton dress.

"How was he killed?" she demanded.

"Poisoned."

She grimaced. "Who did such a thing?"

"They don't know. Not yet."

I sensed movement over by the doorway. I turned in time to see two men come into the room silently, burly young men who moved like big cats. They leaned against the wall inside the door. One of them spoke to her in a fast colloquial Spanish I could not catch even one word of. She answered him with an explosive anger.

"Two of my sons," she said contemptuously. "You worked for Jass?"

"Yes."

"He told you if he died to come to me to give me something?"

"No."

"It does not matter, I guess. Did I ever ask for anything? No! He gave because it was his wish." She stopped and tilted her head. "Then why are you here?"

"I am trying to find out who killed his wife and killed him." I hesitated, then said, "He mentioned you to me once."

Her face beamed. "Yes? What did he say?"

"That you were a very serious thing to him a long time ago."

"Oh yes. My God, I was beautiful! Who could know it now? He was a man. He had wildness. You know? And deep feelings for me. I could have made him marry me, I think. Such a mistake." She sighed, then gave me that intent look again. "Who is this woman with you?"

"This is Miss Webb. My name is McGee. Her brother was killed by, perhaps, the same people who killed Jass."

Her face darkened. "So you think I would know something. Would I hurt such a man? He was *good* to me! Who forced him to give money for the child? No one! He loved her as I do. Did he not take her into his house? She married a good man. Always she gave money for clothes, school, sickness, everything. Even such a big kitchen now, as I have never seen before. He thought of her like a daughter. I have letters from him, saying she is his daughter. He trusted me. I would not hurt . . ."

The hard flow of Spanish from behind me interrupted her. I have a reasonable gringo grasp of the tongue, but when they do not want you to understand, all you can hope to do is pick up the infrequent and unrelated word. She listened to it, looked dubious and then angry. She responded. The young man spoke again. She answered in a softer tone.

I said, "How did Dolores feel about him?"

"With love," Amparo said with great dignity. "What else for the father?" She bit her lip, glanced at her son and said to me, "No one knows of you coming to see me?"

It is a question that rings all the bells. It was extraordinarily clumsy, and it was obvious her son had asked her to ask it. But on the other hand, nearly everything thus far had been clumsy. Murder is not a game for amateurs, for an illegitimate house servant and her half-brothers. I was so busy fitting pieces together I took too much time. My answer was late. "Sheriff Buckelberry sent me here," I said.

It was late and clumsy and it sounded just as false as her question. Incompetence is contagious.

Isobel sensed what was going on and came in too fast and hearty, saying, "Oh yes, the Sheriff knows we've come to see you."

I heard a movement, looked around and saw that the boys were gone. The back of my neck felt chilly. Amparo looked puzzled. It was obvious to me she had no part in whatever had happened.

"Do your sons live here?" I asked politely.

"Eh? No, not those two. Charlie and Pablo. They come to visit, oh a month ago maybe. Out of work, I guess. They are in Phoenix. Canario. From my first husband. That name we gave to Dolores too. I have three little girls name Sosegado. Senor Canario died. A fine man. Esteban Sosegado my husband now, he is in bed for the rest of his life, in the back room. A tractor fell on him. There is the insurance. We manage. If Jass left anything, it would be easier now. But if he did not . . ." She shrugged expressively.

"You do have Jass's letters?"

She drew herself up. "But of course!"

"Could I see one?"

She got up without a word and left the room. Isobel gave me a nervous look. "Is there going to be trouble?"

"I don't know. Don't worry about it."

Suddenly we heard her yelling somewhere in the back of the house. Moments later she came storming back in, rigid with anger, the tears running down her copper face. "Gone!" she said. "Everything. The bah-kus is empty. The letters, the pictures of us smiling and happy. The picture of Jass holding little Dolores in his arms. All gone. Who could do such a thing?"

I could get nothing else from her. She was too upset over the loss of treasures. But she did call goodnight to us as we walked toward the church and the single street of Burned Wells. We walked back to the store. The lantern still hissed, but there was no one around. There was an eerie silence in the still cold air of the night village. I got Isobel into the car and got behind the wheel and turned to her and took hold of her hand.

"There can be some trouble," I said in a low voice. "I didn't like the looks of that pair. I didn't like that question. I am going to leave here in one hell of a hurry, so hang on tight. If I yell to you to get down, get right down onto the floor under the dash."

"A-All right."

I started it up, swung it into a skittering U turn, and aimed it back the way we had come. I reached for the lights and then changed my mind. I could see the pale straight road across the flats by starlight. It was an earnest little car, and I took it right up to the outer edge of control. I expected her to yelp, but she sat braced beside me. I didn't tell her what bothered me. I could see a faint ground-level haziness off to the right of the road, parallel to it. With almost no wind at all, it could be the dust a previous vehicle had kicked up.

I had to drop it way down when I hit the slope, winding up through the rock maze. I had good night vision by then, good enough to look ahead and see where a heavy duty pickup truck, lights off, blocked the road completely. She saw it too. I heard her gasp. They'd picked a good spot, steep rock on both sides. I hit the brakes, banged it into reverse, stuck my head out the window and went down the winding slope backward at a crazy speed. There was one hell of a crack, and a sharp peppery stinging on the back of my steering hand and the back of my neck. It startled me enough to put me off. I banged rock and came back onto the road, then went off the other side, pumped the brakes, nearly rocked it over, came back onto the road again and into a curve and missed the curve, slid it backward onto a ridge to a grinding stop, rear wheels lifted clear of the ground.

I clamped down on her wrist and dragged her out my side. The starlight seemed all too bright on that slope. I hustled her directly away from the road toward a towering mass of jumbled rock and deep shadows. She grunted and struggled and lurched along in her high heels. In heavy shadow I pulled her down beside me, and then squatted on my heels and looked back. Just as I had left the car I had glanced at the windshield, seen the hole punched in my side of it, almost dead center. The dazzle of cracks radiating from the punched hole had made the rest of the windshield, except way over on her side, almost opaque. She was fighting for breath. I looked back along the slope and saw the alarming distinctness of the tracks we had made across the spill of windblown sand. We had to move along, and fast, and across rock. I reached and pulled her shoes off, snapped the high heels off them and gave them back to her.

"Try to manage with these. We've got to move."

She was beginning to please me. She was handling herself well. We went back through shadows and in and out of patches of starlight. I heard one of them call and the other one answer. It sounded too damned close. We were working our way around to the back, out of sight of the road and the car. We came to a slope of rock I thought we could manage. I had her grab me by the belt with one hand, and clamber along behind me. I went diagonally up the long slope. Fifty yards of it, I guessed. I clambered over the top edge into a broad pocket of sand perhaps forty feet wide and sixty feet long, roughly oblong, slightly dished, the sand paled by the night light, the reddened rocks of day stained black.

I looked back and saw the wink and swing of a flashlight along the path we had taken. It would end at the rock slope. They would come up. And this was their country, not mine. They had the guns. I had a woman, and she was gasping for breath. Rough slopes of stone rimmed two sides of the basin. They could be climbed. They went up about thirty feet. The third side was a sheer cliff, just as high. There was a cave mouth in the cliff, narrow and tall.

I said to her in a low tone, "Now do exactly as I tell you."

I had her walk beside me, taking long strides, right to the mouth of the cave. It looked deep. I found a dead branch on the sand and picked it up. We walked backward, in our own footprints in the loose sand, back to the edge of the pitch we had climbed. I looked over the edge and saw that we weren't going to make it. They were dark shapes coming up the slant too swiftly. I saw a tiny fleck of light on metal. But I had to give it a try. I sent her running to where the loose rocks looked easiest to climb and told her to head on up. I backed along after her, wiping out our tracks with broad strokes of the branch. But at any moment a head would come over the edge and we would be in plain view.

"Hold up!" one of them said sharply. I heard it a little after they did, a distant clatter of a noisy engine.

The voices of the Sosegado boys carried well in the stillness. "Be old Tom coming back from Quintana," one said. "Goddam pickup right in his way."

"You stay put. Don't climb up there. I'll go move it."

I blessed old Tom and brushed my way back to the rocky slope. I discarded the branch and climbed up. She was at the top. The stone formation there was as if some giant had picked up a loose double handful of hundred ton dominoes and stacked them there in a jumbled pile. There were a thousand hiding places. I hurried her along to one and told her to stay put.

"What are you going to do?"

"If it doesn't work out, worm yourself back into the smallest deepest place you can find, and don't make a sound. Sooner or later Buckelberry will come looking. Stay alive."

I circled and came back to the top of the cliff overlooking the cave. Using great caution I got a look at the man on the slope. He was crouched there, a red cigarette end against a burly shadow. I moved back until I was directly over the cave. I could see our footprints. They looked convincing. I felt around and located three rocks. A fifteen pound shard about eighteen inches long, and two rough chunks the size of softballs. I had heard the pickup start. He kept it in a low gear. In a little while the sound stopped as he got it off the road. The noisy engine came closer. It stopped straining and went into a rackety idling sound, and I heard voices over the sound of that engine. It started up again and chugged off through the night toward Burned Wells.

I stayed down. The human mind is strange. Scared as I was, I wanted to laugh. A woman, a cave, flight, an arsenal of murderous stones. A hundred thousand years of human progress. I could see a little cartoon of myself dragging Isobel off by her hair. I imagined she would talk about the hostility syndrome.

I did not risk another look down the slope. A silhouette against a starry sky can catch the eye. I heard a clink of metal against rock. Then low talk. They were closer together than before. I could not hear what they were saying. Their basic plan, as I imagined it, seemed sound. How many times can they make you inhale cyanide? So kill the nosy couple, drag them down and dump them into the back of their car. Pull it off the rocks. Knock the blurred windshield out with a stone. Drive it down to the valley floor and across country. Push it into a narrow arroyo, cover it with rocks and brush. And be in bed before the sun comes up.

When one spoke again, the voice was alarmingly close.

"Run right into that cave, Pablo."

"With a gun, maybe?"

"Had a gun, he'd wait in those rocks below to bushwhack us."

"Pretty big mean-lookin' man, boy."

"I seen him too. Hey! You in there. You and the girl come on out, nobody gets hurt."

They waited. The silence was intense.

"Then I come in shooting."

"Charlie, maybe it goes right on through."

"Give me that light. I'm going on in."

I had wormed back from the edge slightly. I took the big shard in both hands and came up onto my knees near the edge. I raised the stone high above my head, then hurled it down onto the one who was right beneath me, shining his light into the cave, his body crouched and cautious. The other one was about fifteen feet back, and he was very very good. As I was hurling the rock downward, he took a pot shot from the hip. The rock was about even with my chest when the slug hit it and whined away into darkness. I felt the impact in my hands just as I released the rock. I went rolling backwards without delay, wondering if the shot would send my target hopping back out of range. But as I rolled back, I heard a heavy, moist and somewhat hollow sound, as if a ripe pumpkin had been dropped on a cement floor.

I kept flat. He had no way of knowing I had not taken the slug in some small degree. Or even seriously. When the angle is correct, they will ricochet nicely off skull bone.

There was silence. I heard a groan of anguish and heartbreak. Suddenly a wild voice yelled, "You kilt him, you son of a bitch! You smashed my brother's head, goddam you!"

"Go home, Pablo. This is more than you can handle, boy."

There was another silence. From further away he yelled, "I'm going to gut-shoot you!" He was moving back to get a better angle at me. I snaked my way to where the stones were plentiful, and with great eagerness and considerable alarm, I kept the air full of stones, arching them high, aiming them where I thought he had to be. I scuttled ten feet to the side and risked a look. He was heading up the slope we had climbed, the slope above the sandy area. I had a good rock and I took aim. It bounced off his hip and sent him sprawling, but even as he fell he managed to get a shot off. A shot close to the head neither whines nor whistles. It makes one audible little explosive huff, very brief and very persuasive. I rolled away and threw another stone into his area. Scrambling swiftly, I picked a different place to take a

look over the edge. He had come back down the slope of
loose rock. He was crossing the sand. He went cat-like down
the solid pitch of rock below the sand, after stopping for a
moment near the body, out of my line of vision. He went
quite a way down, then turned and stopped, partially flattened against the slope.

"You hear me up there?" he called.

"I hear you just fine."

Sounding much more calm and under control, he said, "I'm
not crazy. You get no more chance to chunk me in the
head with a stone."

"So go away."

"You'd like that fine. Come dawn I'm coming up after you.
You killed my blood brother. I make you a promise, man.
You think about it all night. While you're gut-shot and dying
in the morning, you can watch me with your woman."

"Your mouth is big, Pablo. Just like your brother's."

"You can't make me sore now, so I come up there and
you have a chance of busting me with a rock. I got a place
where I can watch this hill, this whole side of it, and you
can't get down the back side of it. I see good in the nighttime, man."

We had been raising our voices at first, but now they
found a natural level in that desert silence.

"Which one of you brave boys killed Mona Yeoman? You,
or this cat-meat brother up here?"

"You don't make me sore, man. I killed her. Good shot,
huh? Not this rifle gun. What I was going to do, I was
going to move it just a hair, and put the next one into you.
Save everybody a lot of trouble. But the round I used on
her, the casing split and the shell case stuck in the chamber,
and it pulled the catch off the ejector."

"You boys were real bright. You couldn't do anything
right, could you?"

"It's going to be all right from now on, man."

"Is that what your half-sister says? Is that what Dolores
keeps telling you?"

"Doe figured it out pretty good."

"She's as stupid as you are, Pablo."

"You think so? What Doe told us, maybe Mona hired
you to kill the old man. That's why Mona had to die first,
but he shouldn't know she was dead, or maybe he'd make
out a new will before we could get to him. You think that's
stupid?"

"Killing people is always stupid."

"Doe isn't stupid. Look, she found out from Mona the best way we could grab that professor. It had to look like she went off with him, right? And he told us where Mona was going to take you, to that cabin. That made a good place, right? You should hear him, that man with all the big words, making little smiles at us, saying we shouldn't. But the last three minutes before we blew the rocks down on him, he spent those three minutes screaming."

"You've got a lot of class, Pablo. A lot of brains. Just like your pal Pompa. Just like that trash you sent on that airplane ride to El Paso. You're as dead as your brother, but you don't know it yet."

"Don't you worry about me. Everything is fine. I kill you both and hide you and go away a couple years. Doe has one smart lawyer, with all the proof about Yeoman being her daddy. I'll bury you and I'll bury my brother Charlie. She'll be rich, man. I can come back in a couple years and get in touch real careful."

"She won't be around, Pablo. And she won't be rich. She took the old man some coffee. Buckelberry's checking out where she got the strychnine. Probably from you boys. The ranches use it for vermin, don't they?"

The stars were bright. A dog-thing hollered a hundred miles away. Somebody walked over my grave. "You so smart, man. Who saw Doe? Nobody!" But there was some defiance there, of the kind that comes from uncertainty, perhaps from fear.

I did not understand these people. Did they think themselves involved in some sort of crusade? A man, his wife, her lover, one hired assassin and one of the brothers—all dead. What turns on this kind of a bloody engine? This Pablo wanted to boost the score from five to seven. If the state could be depended upon to exact its own variety of jungle justice, seven would become nine. And for what?

"Pablo?"

"Too bad it won't be a knife for you."

"I just wonder about something. Dolores knew he was her father. She worked for them, for Jass and Mona. For years. Then she left and got married. Then all of a sudden . . . all this starts."

"You bet your ass, man. It starts good."

"She got hold of you boys to help her."

"Help her get rich. Why not?"

"But wasn't Yeoman good to her?"

There was a chilling cackle of laughter from him. "So good, man. So real good. That's why, man. How much good can you stand?"

I knew I couldn't get any further in that direction. He had stopped making sense. "Where's Mona's body?"

"They'll find it. They can't help finding it."

"Let me ask you one more thing. It was pretty dark in your mother's place. I couldn't get a good look at you and your brother. But I had the feeling I'd seen you before."

"We move around pretty good," he said, very casually. "I saw you good through that scope. Six power. I had those hairs crossed on your belly. No wind at all. Five hundred yards."

"Were you parked a little way down the street that day I visited your sister?"

"Man, you dream it, don't you?"

"What difference does it make now, Pablo?"

After a long silence he said, "She like to kill us both that day, coming to see her in the daytime. Charlie tells her about how we got Pompa, how good he is with a knife. She cried some. Imagine that? She *cried* over that old man."

I had been feeling cautiously around in darkness and found a stone that fit my hand very nicely. It was a little too heavy to throw in normal fashion, but I could heave it stiff-arm like a grenade. It was a very long chance of doing any harm, but any chance was worth taking. The angle was bad. He was perhaps thirty yards away down the slope of rock. I would have to come up a little to do it, risking a momentary silhouette.

I counted to three and came up and threw. An instant after release, as I was already dropping back into cover, I heard the shot and felt a dirty little tug against the fabric right at the point of my shoulder. A tug and a faint impression of heat. He was dishearteningly good. I heard my stone clack against the solid rock and bound on down to the foot of the pitch. He called to me a few times. I kept silent, hoping to con him into thinking he had hit home, hoping he would come up to take a closer look. He stopped calling. I heard a sound further away. I wormed forward and looked and saw him in the starlight, thirty feet from the bottom of the slope, walking directly away from it. He walked to a knoll about a hundred and fifty yards away, and I lost him as he started up it. He had a good place. We would have to come down into the flats if we left the bigger hill. Unless it clouded over, hardly possible, we'd be bugs on a tabletop for that handy-dandy rifle. It was about all the proof I needed that we couldn't get down the other side of our fortress.

As I rolled up onto hands and knees and turned away from the edge, I turned directly into an impact of animal warmth that nearly jumped my heart right out of my chest. She had moved like a spook. Silvery highlights on the moist of an eye, wet of underlip, glad warm exhalation of her breath.

"All that shooting and yelling," she whispered.

"If I can't trust you to do exactly as I tell you . . ."

"Please. I thought maybe I . . . maybe I could help . . ." She dropped the sharp stone she held. It clattered between us. I led her back away from the edge and we hunkered down. I didn't want to be in the way if he tried a blind one just for luck. I told her where he was, and what had happened to the other one. She had worked her way close enough to hear most of my little chat with brother.

"What can we do?" she asked.

"I don't know. We have to think of something. We have to have a surprise for him. When he comes up here at dawn he won't make any stupid mistakes. He'll be cold about it."

"The other one had a gun too."

"And he took it along. I heard him set it down on the slope. It slid a little and he grabbed it."

I sent her off to circle around and wait for me at the top of the incline she had climbed previously, the loose stones above the sand bowl where the man lay dead.

I looked down at the darkness of him sprawled against the sand. I lowered myself over the edge, kicked myself away from the sheer wall and dropped, rolled quickly close to the wall, just in case. Charlie had not been a fastidious boy. Even in that cleansing desert air, stronger than the effluvium of death was a lion-cage smell about him, bringing an atavistic prickling to the back of my neck. Scent of the enemy slain.

I was after tools. Close to the cave mouth I saw a small shadow too orderly in outline to be something from nature. I went to it and discovered that it was the flashlight, a cheap one in a black metal case. I backed into the cave mouth and aimed it at Charlie-boy's head and punched the button. As my stomach took a slow backflip, I heard Isobel's shallow gagging cough. I shoved the flashlight into my pocket and waited for the slow return of complete night vision. Then, with all the assurance of a housewife trying to pick up a dead garden snake, I went through his tight pockets. The only things that seemed useful were his pocket knife and the broad leather belt that held up his soiled jeans. When I rolled him over to get at the belt buckle, trapped gases bubbled from his throat.

I went blundering up the slope in great haste to get away from him. Isobel was waiting at the top. We went back into the giant tumble of rock and went through and around it to a place where there was so much rock between us and the distant brother, I could slowly unpucker. They use slow motion strobe light camera stuff to show what modern slugs do to flesh. They use gelatin of the right consistency. I remember those pictures too clearly, it seems.

We sat on a rock step leaning back against an armchair back of slanted rock. "How do you feel about . . . killing him?"

"That's a goddam fool question."

"I'm sorry. I just . . . feel strange with you because you did it."

"Let's say mixed emotions, honey. There is a very small hot feeling of satisfaction, because he had a gun and I had a stone, and I tricked hell out of them with a very simple device. Then there is a kind of sadness about the waste. And some irony, I guess. Also, a little bit of a sick feeling, like the kid after shooting the sparrow."

She put her hand on my arm. "I'm glad it's all those things. I'm glad you try to be so honest."

"Stay here. I'm going to take a look at this edge of the drop."

It was a sorry look. We were on a butte-like formation where one side had spilled away, like a footstool with dirt banked against one side of it. A twelve-story footstool, with about an acre of jumbled rock on top of it. I stood near the edge and, looking down, I could make out quite a bit of the curving road. I saw my beetle car down there, backed off the curve, with the pickup truck parked off the road about twenty feet from it. I had the feeling I could spit that far. I got down on my belly and looked over the edge at several places. Not a chance anywhere.

I went back to her. She sat hugging herself. The sun heat

was beginning to leach out of the rock, and the night was cold.

I sat close to her and put my arm around her. "We've got to trap him somehow, Iz."

"If we can find a place, maybe, where he can't use the gun?"

"And can't smoke us out. And where we can rig a surprise for him."

We went looking, prowling our huge rocky playpen. She called softly to me. I went over and found her staring dubiously at a triangular opening between two huge stones. It was at ground level, and small. I stretched out and shone the light into it. It looked roomy. I crawled in. After crawling three feet, I found that it opened up nicely. It wasn't a neat cave. It was just an accidental space in tumbled rock, the floor of it at a thirty degree angle, the inside all corners and angles and cantilevered protrusions. It went back about fifteen feet, and at the back of it, around a little corner, was a place big enough for one person to hide out of sight of the entrance. It was refuge, and also a potential trap.

So we armed it. It took a couple of hours of work. She had some pleasantly bloodthirsty ideas. She held the light while I cut the dead man's belt into long thin strips. If man is the most dangerous hunter, he is also the most dangerous game. I searched our front yard and found a length of dry tough fibrous wood as big around as my wrist. I whittled it clean and worked it firmly into a crack off to the side of the entrance, just where it widened out. It extended across the entrance. I tied our leather line to the end of it, ran the line up to a jutting finger of stone and made it fast with a temporary slip knot. Then I put her up there on the knot, and I braced myself and bent the tough wood up until it was above the entrance. When the line had been refastened to hold it in that position, I slowly released my pressure on the weathered limb. The leather held, so tight it thrummed if you touched it.

It was a nervous-making thing to crawl under. I went out and cleared signs away from our entrance, but not too carefully. This was a reverse of the other trick. I tore the sleeve of her suit jacket and plucked a pale thread and caught it into the edge of rock at the entrance. He would see it by dawn-light, if he was a careful tracker. I could assume he was.

Though I did not expect him to try to sneak up in darkness, I rigged an alarm. I wedged a stick across the entrance, as I came back in, one he would have to remove, and carried a line back and looped it over a lip of rock. To it I tied the metal parts of the dismantled flashlight, like a wind chime. The slightest movement of the stick made an audible jangle.

After we had assembled some throwing stones of the proper heft and size, there was nothing more we could do. Without the flashlight, the cave was a total blackness. We rehearsed the positions we would take, then we stretched out on the floor on the slope, our feet braced. I held her. The cold was getting to her. The position was awkward and uncomfortable. After a little while I shifted us. I took my jacket off. I lay at the foot of the sloped floor, my back against stone. I pulled her down against me, wrapped my arms around her and worked the jacket over us.

"Better?" I asked her.

"I think so," she whispered. She was still shuddering with cold. She dug closer to me, face in my neck, arms around my waist. She smelled of vanilla. The treat after the movies in the childhood long ago. After a long time she stopped shivering.

Then it was the catalyst things, of course. All of them. Night, death, fright, closeness, the security of the den. Male and female in the most primitive partnership of all. This was a twisted virgin, frightened by men, sex, pleasure, wanting— thinking it all a conspiracy of evil against her. But now there was a greater fear. There with mingled breath I felt her awareness grow. Her hands held tightly. Slowly her breathing deepened, with a little catch at the peak of each inhalation. Her body heat increased. I knew that at my slightest aggressive movement, it would all drain out of her. If I could pretend not to be aware, then it could all keep building for her. But clamped there together as we were by the pitch of the floor, aroused by her closeness, I could hardly hope to conceal my increasing physiological awareness of her, and I was afraid that as it became all too evident to her, it would chill her. I noted the exact moment of her realization. She stopped breathing entirely. Her whole body tightened. And then, as she took a breath, there was an indescribable softening, a slow flowering of her hips, as though her thighs rolled outward. I moved my hand to the small of her back, and she gasped, and there was a strange and almost imperceptible tremor of her hips, a moth-wind flutter, subtle and sensuous as the final stage of Polynesian dance. She gasped. I found her soft mouth, and for long seconds her mouth was as sensuous and welcoming as her body, and then the old fears took her and she stiffened and turned her head away, pushed at me and said, "No. Oh no."

I released her at once. I sensed that it surprised her. With a wary caution she let the upper half of her body rest against me once more, her hips at a sedate distance. I adjusted the jacket.

I patted her shoulder and said, "Iz, if we get out of this. If I get you out of this. If you're ever in my arms again. Just one word will do it. Every time. No. That's all you have to say. No. And it stops. So don't say it as a nervous habit. Say it when you mean it. No. There's nothing wrong with my hearing."

She thought it over. "But I always thought . . . that men . . ."

"The ravening beast? Don't arouse him? Every man a rapist? Baby, that's just propaganda. There are some dull-witted boys like that, but very few men. Being denied can make me a little irritable. But I don't have to work it out by being aggressive. Just that little word. No. It works. And you can say it at any point you want, right up to the moment when we are, excuse the expression, coupled. From then on it's Molly over the windmill."

She shuddered. "I couldn't. I really just couldn't." She thought for a little while more. "But just this much can be sweet, I guess. I never realized before. But I think it would be . . . dangerous to experiment, Travis."

She yawned so widely her jaw creaked. In another few minutes she drifted off to sleep, collapsing slowly against me.

fourteen

I AWOKE with a jolt that startled her awake. She turned and stared at the visible grey light at our entrance, then scrambled away from me. I crawled to the entrance, checked the triggered club, wormed under it and looked out at the first of day. The sun was not up. The grey of that light and the reddish tone of the huge rocks made of it a purple world. I felt an inexplicable depression. This was the foolish end of all the foolish things, in a purple place for dying. I was too far from the bright water and the bright boats. My luck was gone. When his bullet hit the stone instead of my chest, that was the last of it.

I had not told Isobel the thing I feared most. I was afraid that he would find our burrow, study it, and then go down to the truck and come back with a few sticks and blasting caps. I dismantled my alarm system. We wouldn't need it from now on. It was a terrible temptation to go on out, but he could be thirty feet away, ready to blow my head apart. I went back in and turned and put my finger to my lips. In the vagueness of the reflected grey, I saw the terse nod of her head.

Our planning seemed childish. Rabbity. I was stiff and sore from sleeping against rock. Twenty minutes seemed an eternity. The grey light turned slowly to pink, and the pink began to change to gold when I heard a clack of loose stone not far from our entrance. Soon I heard one crunching footstep. I expected him to call out, but he made no other sound. As the light brightened, more of it came in from overhead, two small patches which filled the cave with a muted glow of early light.

Suddenly I heard a scurrying and a scrambling and a muttered curse. It gave me the wonderful feeling that help had arrived in time. Then there was an almost continuous chirring noise. He was throwing stones at something, kicking sand at it. The something came gliding silently into the cave, head high, and stopped just inside the entrance, in the area of brightness there, and coiled. The tail danced and chirred. The forked tongue took flickering samples of the air. Isobel Webb screamed with total terror.

He was a four footer, as big around as the woman's forearm. There was no need to motion Isobel back. She had gone as far back as she could get, wedging herself around the small corner back there. I snatched up the stick previously wedged in the entrance. The hardware was gone, but the line for the alarm system was still fastened to it.

Rattlesnakes cannot strike beyond their own length. Their eyesight is bad. I had backed my way up off floor level, feeling for footholds in the stone stacked to the side of the entrance, moving up to where the rawhide trigger kept the stout club bent upward over the entrance where the man would have to come through. I quickly fashioned a slip-knot loop in the line fastened to the stick I held, and I bent over and delicately fished for the snake. His head swayed. I got it over his head on the second try.

Just as I yanked it tight, and got the scaly squirming furious length partway off the floor, Sosegado fired four fast shots into the cave. The muzzle blast was so deafening, I knew he had poked the rifle into the entrance and fired it. Slugs whined and clattered around on the walls and ceiling. I saw that Isobel had not been hit. She peered around an edge of rock.

I gave her a maniacal grin to reassure her. As I stepped up and back, moving higher, getting set, bringing the convulsive flapping of the snake with me, I gave a long, hoarse, gargling moan. As she stared at me in terror, I moaned again. Holding the snake off to the side and below me, I opened the pocket knife with one hand, getting ready to lay the blade against the rawhide so I could release the club against his head as he crawled in.

Isobel caught on. "You killed him!" she screamed. "He's bleeding!"

I could guess Pablo had some basic infantry training. He knew how to come in. He could see that the snake was not in that daylight area just inside the entrance. He could guess there would be room to stand up. He came in good. He came scrabbling and diving in, rifle first, intending perhaps to roll up onto his feet and fire at the first movement he detected, woman, snake or man.

He came through so fast, I sliced the thong too late. Instead of getting him in the head, the club gave him a mighty swat across the tight seat of his jeans. He squalled with pain and indignation and surprise. The released end of the rawhide stung me across the face, and I lost my footing and fell the four feet down to the cave floor, knife, snake, stick and all. Isobel, rising to the situation, flung a rock with all her strength and caught me right on the kneecap. As I scrambled and stumbled back, trying to brace myself to grab the rifle when he came up with it, I saw the lightning coil of the still tethered snake, the upward strike, saw the big tan triangular head take Pablo just under the chin as he was trying to come up at me. He rocked up onto his knees, his face absolutely blank, reached a slow hand up to touch the snake, then fell heavily onto his side. It took only that long for the venom, carried by the veins and arteries of the throat, to reach his heart and his brain and turn him off forever. Isobel went immediately into violent hysterics. The snake let go of Pablo. It studied him for a moment or two, as though deciding he was too big to eat, then turned and glided through the slack loop and on out of the cave into the morning sunlight. She came yowling, teetering, tipping into my arms, her face as reddened and wrinkled as the face of an angry child.

There were keys in the pickup truck. Halfway to the state road we met the two county patrol cars heading in toward Burned Wells at high speed. Isobel began to bleat again when she saw what they were. As I stood in the dusty road and pointed at the place where they would find the bodies, I saw that the purple look had faded away. Our hill was a dark silhouette against the morning sun. It had been a place for dying, but not for us. Not for McGee, not this time. A violent and horrible slapstick—a whack across the pants, sting of the thong, woman's bad aim with a stone—and then the terrible efficiency of the swift tan snake. . . .

Late on Sunday afternoon, Dolores Canario Estobar sat in Fred Buckelberry's office. She had insisted there was absolutely no need for her to have an attorney. The Sheriff knew it had to be handled very carefully. She was a handsome woman, newly married, pregnant, married to Johnny Estobar who showed promise of eventually becoming a political figure among the Latin American population of Esmerelda County. He had to let her husband be with her. Johnny, bitterly indignant, sat beside his solemn wife and tenderly held her hand. It was a crowded office. Buckelberry, a deputy, a stenographer, the state's attorney, Jass's personal attorney, the Estobars and me.

Her calm and her dignity seemed unshakable. "Sheriff, I guess the way things are, I have to believe it, that Pablo and Carlos did these terrible things. It's so terribly hard on my mother. I was never close to my half-brothers. How many times do I have to tell you all this anyhow? The only thing I can think of, they got in trouble or something in Phoenix and came back here and plotted this crazy plan to make me rich, thinking that if I got Jass's money they could get a lot of it from me. I've always known I was his daughter. Mona never knew it. Yes, I worked in his house, but I didn't resent him for it. I could have had a lot more education. He would have paid for it. But I quit. He was good to me. I didn't love him, but I didn't resent him. He was being fair in his own way. A lot of men would have done a lot less."

"You knew about the letters your mother had?" Buckelberry asked gently. "And the pictures?"

"Certainly. One of my half-brothers obviously took them. They were wild reckless boys. God knows what they were thinking. Maybe they thought they were helping me. Such a stupid, stupid plan. I know your people have been searching my house, Sheriff. I wouldn't even know what strychnine looks like."

"But you did go to Jass's house shortly after noon on the day of his death?"

"Yes! I've *told* you that. He called me up. He *asked* me to come over. I *went* over and he was *gone*. They can tell you that at his house."

"Do you have to keep asking her the same things over and over?" her husband demanded.

"I don't think she wants to refuse to answer," the Sheriff told him. "Now, Dolores, you see the little problem you leave us. If a person were very clever, they would go over, Yeoman would let them in. They would pour him a cup of coffee—someone who knew his habits well. They would poison him and leave and go a short distance and wait and then go back to the house as though just arriving. That would account for them being seen in the neighborhood, if anybody saw them and remembered."

"Do I have to prove myself innocent?" Dolores demanded haughtily. "I thought it was the other way around for most people."

"How do you imagine your brothers learned

about the affair between Mrs. Yeoman and Mr. Webb?"

"A lot of people knew about that. They weren't real careful, you know. God, I wish Pablo and Carlos were alive. Then they could give you real answers. All I can do is a lot of guessing. Honest to God, I do *not* want any of Jass's money. We're getting along fine. I'm really happy for the first time in my life."

"Why don't you leave her alone?" Estobar demanded.

I could see the hopelessness in Fred Buckelberry's eyes. Unless he could trap her somehow, she was going to walk away from it. And it was getting easier and easier to believe, even for me, that she'd had no part in it. But something about her did not ring true. She was just too damn controlled. I remembered how she had been on the porch of her house when she had flown off the handle. Blood and iron, fire and pride. She had to really hate the old man to kill him that way. And I had a glimmer of an idea. It would be very rough on her. But I had to believe Pablo called the truth to me through the night. He had been certain I wouldn't live to repeat it.

"May I say something?" I asked Fred. They all looked at me.

"Go ahead."

I cleared my throat and looked upset. "I don't know. I keep thinking there's some kind of a mistake here, Fred. While I was working for Jass we got a little stoned together a couple of times. Talked about everything under the sun. I didn't know him a long time, but he seemed like a pretty good guy. The thing is . . . I don't know just how to say this . . . it's just hard for me to believe Mrs. Estobar here was Jass's daughter, because he talked about her as if . . . well, as if she was another woman in the house, if you know what I'm getting at."

There was a deadly silence, and then she launched herself at me. She wanted to spoon my eyes out on her thumbnails. Her husband got her, held her wrists, her arms out behind her. She bent toward me, and her face was nothing human.

"Yesssss," she said in a dreadful half whisper. "When *she* was away. That filthy old man. That father I adored. He was drinking. He made me drink too. I tried to help him to bed. He forced me, that filthy old man. He didn't know who I was. Drunk! A woman to grab. I had loved him, like a daughter." She straightened, raising her voice. *"He destroyed me! He dirtied me!* Oh, I wrote those tax people. They talked to me any times. I told them every damn thing I could remember

bout every dirty trick I heard him say he did. I told Mona
so she would tell him, so he would sweat and squirm and
sweat. Those boys would do anything I made them do. They
thought it was just for the money. Kill his woman. That
was something else gone. I wanted him to live longer, but I
couldn't wait. He drank it down and patted me on the cheek
and said thank you my dear girl. Isn't that wild? Isn't that
hilarious? Doesn't that kill you?" In a slower voice, looking
around at all of us in a dazed way, she said, "Doesn't that kill
you?"

Her husband sobbed and caught her as she went down. And
not one of us was able to look anyone else in the eye.

* * *

Ten weeks later, on a Sunday night, under a moon almost
full, I was stretched out on a sandy blanket on the small
back beach of Webb Cay. It had been the rarest of all perfect
days. Hot and clear, with just enough of a breeze to keep
the sandflies away. We'd done a little more work on the house
that day. I had cleaned the jets on the cranky kerosene refrigerator and gotten it working with less stink. We'd gone
snorkeling and come back with four fine crayfish, boiled them
up, ate them with tinned butter and Pauli Girl beer. We had
sun-drowsed on the beach, swimming when it got too hot,
then gone into the shadowy old house, into relative cool-
ness, into the big bed where her parents had slept, for a long
lazy game of love and the deep sweet nap until dusk.

I looked out and saw her swimming in, the moon so
bright it almost masked the pale green fire of phosphores-
cence her slow strong strokes created. She came wading up
out of the water, up the shelf of the beach, naked in moonlight, palming her dark sea-soaked hair back with both
hands. I had never seen anyone get so dark so quickly. She
was like a Carib Indian. In the daylight, with the white goo
covering her sensitive lips, she had begun to look like a
photographic negative. She was one even perfect color all
over, without streak or patch, a primitive honeyed bronze.

She came to the blanket and knelt and rolled back on her
calf, and made of my left forearm a Japanese pillow for the
baked nape of her neck. She made a small sound of content-
ment and lay there in a spill of moonlight that turned
the water droplets on her body to a mercury gleaming.

"Long swim," I said.

"Just floating out there, darling. Thinking."

"Of?"

"Oh, of whatever happened to that silly beast who tried to kill herself. Maybe you remember her. The one that had fastened herself to the adored brother. A symbiotic relationship. Feeding off him."

"Vaguely remember her. And I remember a girl who kept saying no."

Warm chuckle. "Oh, *her!* She was corrupted long ago."

After all the hundred details of burial, testimony, insurance, closing her apartment, packing, we had taken off in that sedate old sedan, wandering vaguely east, making few miles in each day's drive, following the narrowest blue line on the map. The journey from Livingston to Fort Lauderdale had taken over two weeks. She insisted on a precise division of all expenses. And in the crickety motel nights, in the woodsy old cabins outside small towns, I let her find her own increments of experimental boldness, right up to where she would say, hoarsely, gaspingly, No. And I obeyed that word immediately and without fail. Had I not done so at any time, it would have set her back to the very beginning. She had to know that it would work, would always work, and that it was her option. After a time the tops of her sensible little pyjamas could be shucked, and nights later the bottoms. Some days, in the old car, she would be sensuously humid, sloe eyed, half asleep all day. Other days she would be wound taut, jabbering, chattering, laughing, turning her head with quick motions. I offered her no juvenile substitutes, no cheap devices, because I sensed that her timidity was such that she would settle forever for any half measure afforded her.

I was just fine. Just dandy. Aside from a perceptible hand tremor, chronic indigestion, too many cigarettes, a gaunted face, the feeling that my lower belly was full of scrap iron and a tendency to leap out of my skin at any unexpected sound, I was peachy.

It was her demon and her battle. It was a precipice, and her knowledge that she could stop it at any time gave her the boldness to approach ever closer to the edge. On a sticky night in the X-Cell Motel on the east bank of Mobile Bay, the brink crumbled away under her hesitant footstep. With a soft harsh almost supersonic shriek, like a gaffed rabbit, she fell. We stayed there three days and nights. Clothes were clumsy devices you put on to walk down the road to eat.

We ate like barracudas. We slept twined in the deep innocence of the slumber you remember from childhood. We could look at each other and start laughing for no reason. Roughhouse could turn to passion, to sweetness, to comedy, to passion again.

"How about this here girl right now?" I asked her. "Do much thinking about her while you were floating out there?"

"I've been thinking about her for days," she said. She rolled toward me, bracing herself on her elbow. The moon was slightly behind her, making a furry silver line that followed the deep cleft at her waist, then rose into the full and astonishing curve of her hip. I traced the line with my fingertips. All essential meaning can exist within that ripe convexity. All importance. Or, with an implicit irony, it can be all of cheapness and abuse. The gift is in the manner of the using.

"Reach any conclusions?"

"I've boiled them all down, sort of. Trav, darling, when I was a skinny brown kid racing around this little island, I had a sense of my own rightness. I had a feeling of access to life, as if it would all open up for me, in its own time. God knows how or why it soured, or why I slammed all the doors, why I had such a conviction of evil. Maybe a psychiatrist could track it down. But now it's like it used to be for me. I'm alive once more. And that is a gift from you, of course. But certainly not because you were being terribly terribly generous about everything."

"Wasn't I?"

She snorted. "A very clever and very sneaky seduction, McGee. You let me hang myself with my own rope. Philanthropy, you wretch? Ho! What if the figure was a lot less than Greek, dear? Or the eyes slightly crossed?"

"Well, I did suspect certain hidden qualities, Iz. You know, some people have a natural left hook, and some are born with the ability to throw the fast ball, and others can wiggle their ears. I just had the feeling that if you could ever be . . ."

"Hush. Can't you be serious?"

"If you want. It wasn't all acquisition. It just seemed such a hell of a waste of yourself. And I started to like you."

"I can be honest?"

"Please."

"Trav, one very fundamental part of me, the primitive part I guess, the flesh and bones and blood—that part keeps telling me I can't ever let you go, that I have to have you for always, that I must do anything to keep you near me."

"Hmmm."

"Don't get alarmed, dear. All the rest of me says nonsense. We could never make it work, not on any basis. We are different sorts. I intellectualize things. I am really quite a sober and sedate and earnest woman, present appearances to the contrary. You are a very charming pagan, Mister McGee. And I thank you with all my heart for bringing me into my pagan time. I needed it, to counteract all the other. I needed it to swing me back to some kind of a norm, later on. But this life is more near your norm than it could ever be near mine. I am hooked on duty. Some kind of duty. Some kind of energetic worth. It's the Puritan twitch, inescapable for me, and perhaps in some much more subtle way, inescapable in a smaller sense for you too. You keep having to deny things in yourself, but you do it more readily than I."

"More practice."

"No. It is a more fundamental thing than that. Darling, I relish you. I hunger for you. I can't have enough of lovemaking, as you possibly have noticed. I'm grateful to you. But I don't *love* you. You're a friend, showing me a strange country. And now I begin to see the little signs that this is going to end. You've started to think of leaving. No, don't tell me exactly when."

"One of these days."

"I will be desolated. I will cry my eyes out. I'll ache for you. But I will know it has to be."

"What are your plans?"

"I don't know, darling. I'm beginning to get glimmerings of a few. I have to sort them out. I'm going to stay right here, alone. Jigger will be in from Nassau every Monday with supplies. I don't mind being alone. It will be a chance for consecutive thought, without all these constant trivial interruptions. I shall end up doing something terribly worthwhile, Trav. But I shall find a man to share that kind of life. Somewhere. Somehow. I think I know what to look for and how to look, now. But you will be forever dear to me. You know that."

"In time of trouble, you know where . . ."

"Of course, darling." She stretched and yawned in tawny luxury. "Where'll we go, sweetie? Your place or mine?"

"I remember you bitching this morning about your only toothbrush being at my place."

"So be it," she said.

I took her hand and pulled her up and we walked into the water and swam toward the protected cove where my barge-type houseboat, The Busted Flush, swung on two hooks with plenty of scope. When we had arrived at Bahia Mar, she had gotten pretty edgy about staying with me aboard the boat amid so many people who knew me. She knew they would accept her at whatever value she wanted to put on herself, but it made her less certain of what was happening to her, so I put in two days of hard labor checking the boat out for a cruise. Fortunately there was a very fine long-range forecast, so I could risk the Stream as soon as the Flush was ready to go. The little twin diesels are reliable, and she can take a lot more sea than any of the pontoon-type houseboats, of course, but you have to look for better weather than if you were operating a cruiser. She didn't really begin to enjoy the Sybaritic luxury of the craft until we were well on our way toward Bimini.

I shortened my reach and we swam in a perfect unison out to the cove, and to the boarding ladder. I started the generator to give us lights and water. We rinsed the salt off by taking a stingy cooperative shower in the huge stall, to conserve my dwindling supply.

As I was placidly admiring her as she was scrubbing her teeth, she frowned at me in the mirror and said, out of green foam, "What will happen to her?"

It was a question which could come at any time. It was almost ritual for us. The same question and the same answer. It was the ghost we lived with and talked about. We did not talk about the other ghosts, the big blonde wife whose body they found in the pretentious mausoleum Jass Yeoman had built for the disinterred bodies of his parents, and for himself and his wife, or about the screaming brother buried under the rolling crush of broken stone, or the old man flapping his life away amid the wire baskets and week-end specials, or the crushed skull, or the oiled deftness of the snake.

"It's a delicate situation for her. It will be delayed until after the child is born. There could be less heat by then. My guess would be a plea of guilty to murder second. Just for the old man. They don't have enough to go after her on the other two. I hope it's a guilty plea. Then I won't have to go out."

"How long would they give her?"

"Ten years to life, maybe."

She sighed and stared at me, then bent back to her scrubbing. These were our sad ghosts, and they made life sweeter somehow by keeping us aware of what a precarious gift it is. And when life seems sweet, love is an exaltation.

After she had sighed and sighed her way down into her cozy little buzzing sound of deepest sleep—her sign that all that there was to give had been entirely taken—I left the master stateroom and clambered up to the sun deck and stretched out naked under a billion stars. Maybe the talk had done it. Tonight the lovemaking had had that first tart sweetness of impending goodby. And there would be a little more of that flavor from now on.

Maybe, before we parted, I would tell her—or try to tell her—how she, in her own way, had mended me. A different fellow had gone out there to Esmerelda, with the bad nerves and the flying twitches and the guilts and remorses and the feeling of being savagely and forever alone. No guilts this time. Not with this one. Remorse is the ultimate in self-abuse.

So under the stars I let myself think of that old man a little bit. That old Jasper Yeoman. There was the truly terrible guilt, that ever-present knowledge of the incest the world most heartily despises. Perhaps he was glad to die, and perhaps he realized his Dolores had killed him. Maybe he was glad dying came so hard, by her hand. Maybe, in his times of lucidity between the terrible spasms of the poison, he kept himself from saying her name and how she had done it. It would be one kind of penance. And there are never enough kinds. Not for him. Not for me. And certainly not for you, my friend.

JOHN D. MacDONALD

"The king of the adventure novel" John D. MacDonald is
one of the world's most popular authors of mystery and
suspense. Here he is at his bestselling best.

CONDOMINIUM	23525	$2.75
ALL THESE CONDEMNED	14239	$1.75
APRIL EVIL	14128	$1.95
BALLROOM OF THE SKIES	14143	$1.75
THE BEACH GIRLS	14081	$1.75
THE BRASS CUPCAKE	14141	$1.95
A BULLET FOR CINDERELLA	14106	$1.75
CANCEL ALL OUR VOWS	13764	$1.75
CLEMMIE	14015	$1.75
CONTRARY PLEASURE	14104	$1.75
THE CROSSROADS	14033	$1.75
DEADLOW TIDE	14166	$1.75
DEADLY WELCOME	13682	$1.50
DEATH TRAP	13557	$1.50
THE DECEIVERS	14016	$1.75
THE DROWNERS	13582	$1.75
THE EMPTY TRAP	14185	$1.95
THE END OF THE NIGHT	14192	$1.75
THE LAST ONE LEFT	13958	$2.50

Buy them at your local bookstore or use this handy coupon for ordering.

COLUMBIA BOOK SERVICE (a CBS Publications Co.)
2275 Mally Road, P.O. Box FB, Madison Heights, MI 48071

Please send me the books I have checked above. Orders for less than 5
books must include 75¢ for the first book and 25¢ for each additional
book to cover postage and handling. Orders for 5 books or more postage
is FREE. Send check or money order only.

Cost $_____   Name _____

Sales tax*_____   Address _____

Postage_____   City _____

Total $_____   State _____ Zip _____

*The government requires us to collect sales tax in all states except AK,
DE, MT, NH and OR.*

This offer expires 1 June 81   8004